"WELCOME TO
THE LAND OF THE LIVING!"

Cara stood in the open door at the back of the wagon. Slocum propped himself up on one elbow and simply stared at her. Hair spun gold in the sunlight framed her face. Cool, green eyes appraised him. She deftly uncorked a small, brown vial and held it to Slocum's lips.

"Hey, that's awful!" Slocum protested, gagging.

"Of course it is." Cara laughed. "Medicine is *supposed* to taste bad. This is the finest medicine there is. This is Doctor Wong's Virility Potion and Intestinal Eliminant. It cures what ails you, turns you regular as a twenty-dollar watch, and," she continued, her voice lowering seductively, "makes a good man better."

Slocum suddenly began to feel much, much better as he felt gentle fingers slowly caress his chest.

"See?" Cara O'Connell said, "the good Doctor's remedy is working already. A miracle!"

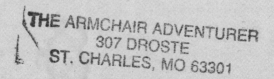

OTHER BOOKS BY JAKE LOGAN

JAKE LOGAN

THE JOURNEY OF DEATH

BERKLEY BOOKS, NEW YORK

THE JOURNEY OF DEATH

A Berkley Book/published by arrangement with
the author

PRINTING HISTORY
Berkley edition/June 1985

ISBN: 0-425-07753-5

A BERKLEY BOOK® TM 757,375
Berkley Books are published by The Berkley Publishing Group,
200 Madison Avenue, New York, N.Y. 10016.
The name "BERKLEY" and the stylized "B" with design are trademarks
belonging to Berkley Publishing Corporation.

PRINTED IN THE UNITED STATES OF AMERICA

THE JOURNEY OF DEATH

1

"We can do it without killing more'n three or four," said the swarthy, scar-faced Henry Nathan. "Anybody want to be counted out because of that?" His dark eyes narrowed as he looked around the tight circle huddled near the guttering campfire, challenging any to tell him he was wrong.

John Slocum spoke up. "No need to kill anybody. We've got this planned good. Unless you enjoy shooting down innocent women and children."

"You questioning my judgment on this, Slocum?" Nathan rose to his feet, hand poised over the butt of his battered Remington. The two men locked eyes, dark ones quickly finding Slocum's cold green ones too much to bear. Nathan broke off the contest of wills and settled back down.

Slocum had shown no sign of nervousness, but he'd been ready to get his Colt Navy out of its holster and firing if Nathan had wanted it that way. Slocum had seen the man's like before and didn't much cotton to him.

When Slocum rode with William Quantrill there'd been men in the ranks who killed for the sheer thrill of seeing their gutshot victim kicking around in the dust, bleeding to death inside. That kind of killing had never set well with Slocum, but he'd been a soldier and had done his share.

Death and John Slocum were no strangers, but he didn't like the sound of Henry Nathan going into this bank robbery saying there'd be bystanders gunned down. If anyone got in their way or threatened them, that was another matter, but Nathan made it sound as if he wanted to see blood more than the greenbacks locked up in the national bank vault down on Paisano Street.

"Don't forget who's the leader of this here group, Slocum." Nathan almost growled now, his courage returning. He looked around the campfire at the others to make sure they backed him up.

Walt Larouche would jump every time Nathan said "frog." He was a pale man in spite of years spent knocking about the South and West. Slocum had heard Larouche had got into trouble down in San Antonio over a Mexican whore, killing three men and wounding two more. It had been Larouche's bad luck that one of the men he'd shot down was a marshal. It was even worse luck that the marshal had been going in the other direction. How Walt Larouche had found his way to this mesquite-fed campfire at Hueco Tanks ten miles outside El Paso del Norte was something Slocum didn't ask or much care about.

The other man, Nails Rawlinson, got his name from being a smithy. With arms damn near as thick as Slocum's waist, Nails looked to be able to pick up a horse when he shod it. Heavy bony ridges covered with eyebrows more like caterpillars wiggled on the man's forehead, giving him a perpetually puzzled expression. Nails was as dumb as he was strong.

"I'm in this because I want to be," said Slocum, carefully choosing his words. He didn't aim to get Nathan riled, but he didn't want to go into El Paso with guns blazing, either. The soldiers bivouacked there might not take kindly to it. As it was, just robbing a national bank might be enough to bring out the troopers, but Slocum counted on them staying out of it, thinking that tracking the Apaches down in Dog Canyon was enough for any man. But shoot one of them and the only place for any of what Nathan called his gang would be over the border and down into Mexico until even the Yaquis couldn't find them. Better just to keep the commotion down to a roar and not get anybody but the local sheriff involved.

"Don't you forget that, either," Nathan said too loudly. In the distance a coyote moaned. The man looked about, his nerves obviously jangled. "Damn sons of bitches," he muttered. "All the time yowling like that."

"When we goin' inta town again?" asked Nails. "The stage ain't due for another couple days. I ast the station-master and he said—"

"You did what?" bellowed Nathan. "I told you to stay out of sight. We don't want anyone knowin' who we are."

"Aw, Henry, I got bored sittin' around and I thought—"

"You never had a thought in your life," Nathan snapped.

Slocum lounged back on his bedroll and tried to ignore the argument. If he hadn't been so down on his luck, he'd never in a thousand years have tied in with these men. For all Nathan's prattling on about the banks he'd robbed and the men he'd killed, Slocum figured him for nothing more than a bag of wind. Slocum preferred to earn his money rather than removing it from other folks' pockets, but times were more than hard for him. He'd drifted through Van Horn and not found any work to speak of. Heading north, he got shot at half a dozen times by ranchers too spooked to talk first. The Mescalero

Apache had been giving everyone a bad time of late, and it paid to shoot first and not bother with damn fool questions at all.

For John Slocum, it had been more than two months since he'd had two nickels to rub together. What living he'd done had been mostly in the desert and off the occasional incautious rabbit or rattler, and he was getting tired of it. For once he wanted to sleep in a bed, knock back a swallow or two of good whiskey, and buy himself a rare steak in a restaurant. If nobody would give him the job he wanted, he'd find employment of his own.

Robbing banks wasn't that far off the trail for him, anyway. Not considering some of the things he'd been forced to do since the War.

"Nothing more to do than get on into town in the morning," said Nathan. "That suit you, Slocum?"

"You're the boss," he said. His tone told the would-be bank robbers exactly what he thought, though.

"Don't go givin' me no trouble, Slocum. I won't stand for it." Henry Nathan's fingers stroked over the butt of his pistol. Slocum almost told him that nervous gestures like that one got men killed, but he kept silent. These three weren't his idea of real highwaymen, but they'd have to do until something better came along. His share of the loot from a prosperous national bank like the one on Paisano Street would keep him in spending money for quite a while.

"How'm I supposed to get in?" asked Nails. His horse had died under the bulky man the day before. "I could steal one over at the Tanks. The stationmaster's got a whole corral of horses for the stage."

"No!" Nathan was emphatic on this, and Slocum had to agree. Better to wait until they got into El Paso before doing the horse thieving. Then it wouldn't matter. Tip their hand too early, though, and half the countryside would be on their necks before they rode up to the bank entrance.

But the furtive looks Nathan kept giving Slocum made

the man suspicious. He had stumbled across the trio, and one thing had led to another. Before long, they had sat down and began discussing how easy it would be to rob that bank. A plum waiting to be picked, Nathan said. He'd already scouted it out, too. Slocum would have chosen his companions in crime differently if the opportunity had presented itself. That it hadn't didn't bother him unduly. He would just have to watch even more carefully for a double-cross.

"You take Walt's horse. Walt, you ride double with . . ." Nathan's words trailed off as he glanced over at Slocum. The cold green eyes again fixed on him, making Nathan edgy. His Adam's apple bobbed a couple of times, then he finished, ". . . with me. When we get into El Paso we can get you another horse. Might all get fresh mounts. We'll have to be ridin' pretty damn hard before they get their wits about them."

"Where we heading after the robbery?" asked Slocum. If the robbery went according to plan, only Henry Nathan and possibly Larouche would be carrying the scrip. To get his share, they would have to meet and divvy up the take.

"Toward Las Cruces through the pass and on the far side of the Franklin Mountains. Then we split up and go whatever way we want."

"But Henry, you said—" began Nails Rawlinson.

"Shaddup." The smithy fell silent and looked sullen, but said no more. Slocum wondered what the dim-witted giant had been about to say. It hardly mattered. He tipped his dusty, sweat-stained hat down over his eyes and pulled his blanket tighter around his body to keep off the cold desert night winds. As long as he stayed alert, he'd be a few hundred dollars richer for a few minutes' work, and then he'd be away from these men.

Dreams of good food in his belly, smooth whiskey rushing down his gullet, and a wanton woman in his bed kept Slocum content all night long.

•   •   •

They'd left Hueco Tanks behind an hour ago and rode into El Paso del Norte just as the sun poked above the hills at their back. The town had grown from a scattering of adobe huts in 1681 to a thriving, incorporated border city in 1873, able to support a bank big enough to make it worthwhile to rob. Slocum figured that the national bank ought to give them a few hundred dollars apiece, maybe more. With any luck, there might even be some of the troopers' money from Fort Bliss there, too, but probably not. The Army kept close rein on their own money and didn't like civilians touching it.

Slocum sighed. It was probably just as well if they went after only the civilian scrip. With a real outlaw band, robbing the fort of its payroll would be the obvious thing to do. With Nathan and the other two, they might shoot themselves in the foot from the excitement of getting near a bank. Slocum didn't relish the thought of having a company of soldiers after him, either. No, just let it be the town bank and not the fort's payroll, though the idea of taking some of that Yankee money appealed greatly to him.

"The damn horse is pulling up lame, Henry," complained Nails Rawlinson. The burly man dismounted and studied the horse's right front hoof. From the way he tended the animal, it was obvious he preferred smithing to bank robbing.

"We're getting there. Just walk the horse for a spell. When we spot another horse, we'll take it. And get down, Larouche. It's too damn hot with you riding behind me."

Walt Larouche climbed down and went to walk with Rawlinson. Slocum said nothing. Already they were bickering. What might he expect when it came time to divvy up the stolen money? Without realizing he even did it, Slocum slipped the thong off the hammer of his Colt Navy to prepare himself for a fight.

"There's a fine-looking pair," said Nathan, pointing to a pair of horses hitched under a crudely lettered sign proclaiming this dusty path to be Mesa Street. "Go take 'em."

Slocum waited while Larouche and Rawlinson stole the horses. His own was well enough rested. Besides, horse thieving rankled him. Bank robbing was one thing, but stealing another man's horse was about as lowdown as you could get. In this part of the country, not having a horse spelled certain death.

The long miles of desert he'd crossed would have been impassable without a sturdy horse. He patted his on the neck and said softly, "Soon enough, old fella, you're going to be dining on oats instead of *chamisa* and sagebrush."

They rode in silence along the streets just stirring with early morning business. The four of them paused outside the bank, exchanging looks. Larouche was frightened. Rawlinson was too dumb to be scared. Nathan looked like he was ready to mow down everyone in sight. And Slocum floated along like a leaf on a stream, not anticipating, not thinking, just moving and ready to respond.

He dropped off his horse and went to the beveled glass front doors of the bank. "Well?" he asked the others. "You coming or not?"

Nathan almost fell off his horse in his haste to join Slocum. The shorter man shoved Slocum aside and slammed hard into the door. It sprang inward, smashing into the wall and breaking a pane of glass.

"This is a stickup!" Nathan yelled. Slocum cringed. This wasn't the way they'd planned it. All of them were supposed to be inside before Nathan announced their intention. Slocum pushed in quickly, pistol in hand— just in time.

A bank guard was lifting a sawed-off double-barreled shotgun. The sight of the .31 caliber Colt Navy unwaveringly pointed at his head caused the guard to reconsider.

"Just slide it over, easy," said Slocum. He hefted the shotgun in his left hand while keeping the guard covered with his Colt. Rawlinson and Larouche crowded in and began babbling about getting the money.

"Shut up!" yelled Slocum. "All right, ladies and gentlemen. Please put your valuables into the sacks as they come around. And you," he said, aiming the shotgun at the teller behind the second window, "keep your hands where we can see them. Nobody'll get hurt."

The snap of command in his voice kept the bank employees from getting any heroic notions. The three customers in the bank—an old geezer already half drunk, a middle-aged woman, and a young cowhand who didn't even carry a sidearm—all stood petrified.

"Hurry it up, come on, come!" shouted Nathan, trying to reassert his control. "Don't take all day. This is the Nathan gang you're dealing with."

Slocum groaned inwardly. If Henry Nathan was trying to do things wrong, he couldn't be doing any better. There wasn't a person in the bank who'd forget that name now.

"Out," said Slocum. "We got enough."

"The vault," said Nathan, his eyes wide. The way he licked his chapped lips betrayed his case of nerves. He was riding on a knife edge and might go over at any instant. "There's more in the vault. Open it, you. Do it!"

"I ... I don't know the combination," the frightened teller said. "And the bank manager just stepped out to—" The man's explanation ended abruptly when Nathan shot him down.

"What'd you do that for?" demanded Slocum.

"He was lying. Nobody lies to Henry Nathan—no, sir. You," the outlaw said, pointing at the other teller, "open the vault."

The teller closed his eyes. Slocum saw the man's lips moving in silent prayer as he prepared to die. Before Nathan got off another shot, Slocum knocked his gun away with the barrel of the shotgun.

"He doesn't know," Slocum said. "Let's take what we can and get out of here."

"He does know, damn it!" raged Nathan, out of control now. "The lying bastard knows how to get the money out of the vault!"

Everything fell apart then. Slocum had taken his eyes off the guard to deal with Nathan. Arms lent strength by stark fear closed around Slocum's shoulders. The guard grunted and heaved, upending Slocum and tossing the tall man off his feet. Slocum dropped the shotgun and kicked out, but the guard's grip was too powerful. The arms around him went limp when the shotgun roared. Blood and bits of flesh dribbled onto Slocum's arms; Nathan had shotgunned the guard in the back.

Slocum saw Nathan's finger tighten on the second trigger. Then reason returned. Nathan saw that, even with a shotgun, he wasn't going to be able to kill Slocum before the man fired that well-used Colt with the worn ebony handle. The trigger finger relaxed.

But the gunfire sounding in the room became deafening. Rawlinson and Larouche had opened fire and cut down the bank customers. The cowboy lay writhing on the wood floor, clutching at his belly. The woman sprawled gracelessly on her back, eyes open and already glazing over in death. The old drunk had pissed on himself in fear and cowered behind a writing table.

"Get the damn money," shouted Slocum, "and let's get out of here!"

As if dazed, Nails Rawlinson went behind the tellers' cages and rifled through the money drawers, stuffing handfuls of greenbacks into his gunny sack. Slocum glanced out into the street. Already the cry had gone up that the bank was being robbed. Getting out of town would be doubly difficult now that Nathan and the others had gone trigger-happy.

"We done it," Nathan said, eyes glowing. "We done it!"

Slocum raced outside and vaulted into the saddle. He put the spurs to his horse before he saw any of the others emerge from the bank. As crazy as Nathan had become, he might decide to come out shooting. If he did, there'd be no way in hell any of them inside the bank would escape alive, but Nathan seemed to know this. Hard on Slocum's heels came his three cohorts, their horses straining, Nathan laughing wildly.

"They're gonna fear the Nathan gang, yes, sir!" the swarthy man cried. "There's gonna be a thousand-dollar reward out on my head 'fore I finish with them!"

Slocum didn't bother telling Nathan how stupid that sounded. For even a ten-dollar reward, there were bounty hunters willing to backshoot any man. Nathan's actions brought more trouble than notoriety, and chances were good he'd end up in an unmarked grave rather than on everyone's lips, like he hoped.

Slocum kept his horse as calm as he could, then he gave up and let his steed have free rein. The animal surged and put its head down, racing for the mountains.

"We're the Nathan gang!" shrieked Henry Nathan, riding alongside up with the other two. "We're the baddest gang in all of Texas!"

A hail of gunfire answered him. The man laughed wildly and began spraying bullets left and right. Slocum looked back over his shoulder and saw that the others put the spurs to their mounts and galloped behind him. He cursed them and he cursed his own foolishness in being so weak. He could have taken out the bank by himself with less fuss.

Now he rode a gauntlet of rifle fire. Men lined the street and levered shells into waiting chambers. Twitching fingers kept the shots from being too accurate, but the hot lead winging by his ears kept Slocum hunkered low and cursing even harder.

Nathan came even with him. The look on the man's face defied description. Slocum had seen men go berserk during the War, forgetting all about their own safety as they made headlong attacks against overwhelming odds. Sometimes they lived. Usually they died.

He wondered how Nathan had survived.

"We done it! We robbed their damn bank!"

A marksman got in a clean shot on Nathan. The man jerked slightly and tiny red rivulets began staining his shirt, just under his right shoulder. But Nathan was so lost in the thrill of robbing and killing he didn't take notice. Slocum bent lower and began spurring his horse. The poor animal's sides heaved and foam slathered along its flanks; getting out of El Paso del Norte was more important to Slocum than being gentle.

A few stray bullets winged their way past Slocum's head, but he stayed low riding the horse's neck and turned the corner around the gap and came out on the west side of the pass. Slocum had to restrain himself to keep from guiding his horse toward the sluggish stream that was the Rio Grande, across the *Chamizal* and over into Mexico. He found himself caught on the horns of a dilemma.

Being away from Nathan and the others was the smartest thing he could do, but Nathan still had the money from the robbery. It wasn't much, but it was better than nothing, and for all the trouble he'd been through, Slocum deserved something.

"They aren't following!" crowed Nathan. "The lily-livered bastards are lettin' us go scot free!"

Slocum wasn't convinced on that. The robbery had come quick and ought to have gone clean. A posse would be less inclined to follow if they hadn't killed those customers. Nobody cared that much about bankers, but when local folks got gunned down, everyone sat up and took note.

"They will," Slocum shouted over the wind rushing in his face. "They'll be after us before the hour's up."

Nathan looked at him and Slocum went cold inside. It didn't seem to matter. For Nathan, the killing had been the important part. Slocum considered turning and putting a bullet into Nathan's head then and there, but the sound of Rawlinson and Larouche so close behind stopped him.

Better to get his share of the money and fade away. Nathan was as crazy as a stewed hoot owl. The sheriff and any posse would find him soon enough. Then Slocum could find his way into Mexico and to points farther south until the robbery and murders faded from local memory.

Slocum reined in a mite and let his horse slow from the breakneck gallop. Panting heavily, the horse stumbled a little. Slocum pulled up even more. Larouche shouted at him, "Ride, damn it! We don't want them to catch us!"

"Won't be anything left to ride if our horses die, now will there?" Slocum dropped down to a slow walk, even though the others weren't inclined to do the same.

He watched as the trio raced on ahead, but he caught up with them less than a mile up the road leading to Las Cruces. Their animals had tired out completely, and the one on which Nails Rawlinson rode wobbled visibly under the man's bulk.

"Keep movin'," urged Nathan. "We can make it."

"Should have planned for more horses," said Slocum. "If the sheriff takes it easy, he'll have us before sundown."

"There, up 'head," panted Larouche, pointing to a creosote bush with a red bandana tied to it. The man galloped toward an arroyo already kicked up with fresh hoofprints. Their horses slid down the sandy bank. Slocum followed the others at a slower pace. They obviously knew where they headed, and he didn't. "He did it. The son of a bitch did it!"

Slocum frowned when he saw the horses in the arroyo, reins leading up to a mesquite bush. Three animals stood pawing at the sand, obviously not liking the hot sunlight beating down on them.

"Where'd those come from?" Slocum asked.

"*I* arranged for 'em," bragged Nathan. "Paid an *hombre* to have 'em staked and ready for us this morning."

Slocum's eyes narrowed. "There's only three horses. There are four of us."

Nails Rawlinson screeched like an old woman when his horse collapsed and died under him. The smithy kicked himself free and stood in the center of the gulley, hands on his hips. "Let's get outta here, Henry. I don't like this place. Damn horse." Nails kicked his dead mount.

The brief second Slocum had turned toward the hulking giant of a man allowed Nathan to draw forth the sawed-off shotgun he had taken from the bank guard. Nathan said, "Three horses is all we'll be needing."

The shotgun blast caught Slocum as he got his Colt halfway out of his holster. He felt the impact of the buckshot, flying off his horse and through the air. Then blackness fell, as surely as night follows day.

2

The flies buzzing around Slocum's face brought him back to a groggy life. He batted weakly at the flies, his hand feeling as if he wore thick woolen mittens. One eye opened. Slocum instantly regretted the effort. The light angling in over the edge of the arroyo hit him straight on and drove a steel knife into his brain.

Slocum rolled onto his side and blacked out from the pain. When he regained consciousness again, a cold wind whipped off the nighttime desert sands. Gingerly, he turned onto his back and stared up at the sky. The crystal-clear air showed the stars to cosmic perfection. Slocum made out the Big Dipper and the North Star and found more pain in his body. With fingers shaking, he pulled his attention from the cloudless sky down to his bloodied shirt.

His chest looked as if a crazed butcher had made sausage out of it. Here and there he spotted the ass end of some of the buckshot poking through his flesh. Slocum gave up trying to squeeze out the lead using only his fingernails. He was too weak, and it hurt too much. Collapsing back to the cold sand, letting the flies light on him, feeling the voracious ants nipping at his legs and bare feet, he tried to get it all straight in his head.

"Nathan shotgunned me," he said aloud, his voice cracked. "Son of a bitch shotgunned me." Details tumbled into place now and his anger mounted. The smithy had distracted him when his horse died, Nathan had lifted the stolen shotgun and pulled the trigger. That reduced the number sharing in the bank loot from four to three. Or had Nathan finished off Rawlinson and Larouche, too?

Slocum tried to sit up, but dizziness drove him flat again. His boots were gone, as were his gunbelt and Colt. Of his horse and tack he saw no sign. Nathan had probably robbed him of those, too, before leaving him to die.

A soft sliding sound turned Slocum cold inside. Tipping his head to one side—all the movement he could do without passing out—he saw a sidewinder slipping gently along the sandy arroyo bottom.

"Go away," he said softly. The snake hesitated, then turned toward him, approaching cautiously, tongue tasting the scent in the air. "I'm not dinner. Go 'way."

A harsher crunching noise came from beyond his range of vision. Whatever caused the sound made the sidewinder stop. It curled into itself, its long, split black tongue testing the air more furiously now. Slocum felt sand cascading onto his face, blinding him as something moved.

"Gotcha, you slithery son of a bitch!" came the loud cry.

When Slocum blinked the sand from his eyes, he saw a curved black metal hook pinning the snake's head to the arroyo bottom. A hand came into his view and grasped the snake firmly just behind the head and picked the wiggling five-foot viper into the air. A burlap bag swung past Slocum's eyes, followed by a piece of rope. The bag, tightly tied with the snake inside and hissing, dropped a few feet away.

"Never mind, Billy," called the man who'd captured the snake. "Someone's already robbed him. Just take the bag with the snake. I'll look at it later."

Boots filled Slocum's world, then they began to recede. "Wait!" he croaked, his voice almost failing him. "Don't leave me. Don't!"

"He's still alive!" came the startled words from down the arroyo. "Why, Mort Thorogoode, you can't just leave him to die like this." The rustle of a woman's skirts came closer.

"Please, help me," Slocum got out. He didn't know if any of these people heard or not. His mouth felt as if all the plantations in the South had filled it with prime long-staple cotton. At least the woman knew he hadn't died.

"He's no good to us, Cara," said the man belonging to the boots still in Slocum's view. "Tore up bad, and look at him: no gun, no boots, no money. Somebody beat us to him."

"Sometimes you make me so mad, Mort. We can't leave him to die."

"Why not?" The man sounded puzzled.

"It's not the Christian thing to do." This provoked loud laughter.

"Cara—or should I say Princess Lotus Blossom— we ain't Christians. Leastways, not good ones."

"Then it's time to start. Help me get him up, Mort." The woman's voice turned colder. "Mort. Do it."

"Sometimes I wonder about you, Cara." Strong hands slipped under Slocum's shoulders and pulled him to a sitting position. He coughed and sputtered and damn near passed out again. With grim determination, Slocum hung on.

The man was all duded up in a dark cutaway coat,

vest with dangling gold chains and sharply creased trousers out of place in the middle of the desert. What struck Slocum as even stranger was the tall silk top hat perched at a jaunty angle. The man held his snake hook in one hand and lightly tapped it into the palm of his other hand. Piercing eyes studied Slocum's wounds.

"Thanks," Slocum grated out.

"Don't talk," the woman said, kneeling beside him. He winced as she pulled away more of the blood-caked shirt to examine his chest. "You caught quite a load of buckshot, from the look of it. Can you stand?"

"I must've died," Slocum said, staring at the woman. "This has to be heaven, and you're too beautiful to be anything but an angel."

She smiled prettily. In the dark Slocum thought she might have even blushed at his compliment. Eyes as green as emeralds peered at him. He read concern but no fright at his condition. She had seen much, this lovely blonde woman.

"How'd you keep from getting ripped apart?" asked Mort Thorogoode. He used his snake hook to lift up one tattered side of Slocum's shirt. "From the powder burns, it looks as if someone shot you at close range."

"Charge must have been bad," said Slocum. "Don't know. Lucky."

"He'll cease being lucky unless we get the pellets out of his chest."

The woman stood and yelled, "Billy! Get yourself over here and help us."

Mort Thorogoode ran an arm around Slocum's shoulders and heaved. Slocum would have fallen on his face if Billy hadn't come along about then to lend a hand. The two men half dragged, half carried him out of the arroyo and over to a gaudily painted wagon.

Another woman sat on the tailgate, feet idly kicking back and forth. Like Cara, she showed no sign of dismay at Slocum's injuries. Her pug nose wrinkled a bit and she said, "Don't go getting blood on the sheets. You know how hard it is to get out."

That was all the introduction John Slocum had to Doctor Wong's Travelling Medicine Show before he passed out again.

Cool, damp compresses lay on Slocum's forehead. He stirred, reached up, and moved the cloth. Only then did he open one eye and look around, almost fearful of what he'd find. His memories were scrambled like a plate of eggs. Of Mort Thorogoode and Cara he remembered only bits and pieces—mostly the sidewinder being stuffed into a bag. But of Nathan and his backshooting cohorts he remembered everything. Clearly.

It surprised Slocum to find his chest bandaged expertly. He took a hesitant breath, then released it. Some pain but not enough to matter. He'd felt worse after a long night of carousing.

"Welcome back to the land of the living," came the musical voice he identified as belonging to the woman.

She stood in the open door at the back of the wagon. Slocum propped himself up on one elbow and simply stared at her. He hadn't thought she was this beautiful. Shoulder-length hair rippled in golden waves as the hot desert winds blew into the wagon. She pulled herself up the final step, shutting the rickety door behind her.

"You weren't all that badly injured," she said.

"Looked bad to me," Slocum answered.

"Looks can be deceiving. Not a one of the pellets went much more than skin deep. I imagine the impact was considerable, but no permanent damage was done." Cool green eyes stared down at him, silently asking for details.

"Not many folks would help out a stranger like you did. Thanks."

"I'm Cara O'Connell," she said.

"John Slocum."

Cara stared at him for a moment, then laughed. "You play the cards close to your chest, don't you?"

"What do you mean?"

"I expected you to tell me all about how you just happened to be left for buzzard bait. Most men would be babbling their fool heads off about it." She laid a cool hand on his brow, then lightly moved her fingers along a flushed cheek. "You have a little fever. Here, take a sip of this."

Cara reached up over Slocum's bunk and took a small brown bottle from a rack. She deftly uncorked it and held the vial to Slocum's lips. He gagged at the bitter liquid dripping onto his lips.

"That's awful!"

"Of course it is," Cara laughed. "Medicine is *supposed* to taste bad. And this is the finest medicine what is. Maybe the finest medicine what ever was." The woman's pale cheeks took on rosy highlights as she swung into the pitch. "This is Doctor Wong's Virility Potion and Intestinal Eliminant. It cures what ails you, gives you relief from catarrh and bleeding gums, turns you regular as a twenty-dollar watch and," she continued, her voice lowering seductively, "makes a good man better."

Cara's fingers worked down Slocum's chest and brushed over his crotch. He felt himself becoming uncomfortably hard at the lovely woman's touch.

"See?" Cara O'Connell said. "The good Doctor's remedy is working already. A miracle!"

The wagon jerked and started bouncing over uneven ground. Slocum fought back a wave of giddiness.

"Where we heading?" he asked. It occurred to him that returning to El Paso was the last thing in the world he wanted. Too many would recognize him as one of Nathan's gang. If the damn fool hadn't announced to the world who was robbing the bank, Slocum would have felt a world better. Even so, enough people would be able to identify one of those holding up the bank.

"That worry you?" Cara asked.

"A man in my condition..." Slocum let the sentence trail off so she could supply whatever explanation she wanted.

"Mort decided to travel up the *Jornado del Muerte* until we get to New Albuquerque."

"Going north through the desert? This isn't a good time of the year to make the trip."

"No time is, but there're enough towns along the way for us to get fresh water." Cara looked at Slocum with cool interest. "The thought of all those Apaches scalping any white man in sight, maybe dying of thirst, certainly being damned uncomfortable doesn't bother you as much as going into El Paso del Norte, does it now?"

"Can't expect you good people to change your plans on account of me," Slocum said. "I do appreciate all you've done for me." He started to sit up, but Cara pushed him back down.

"None of that. You've got some explaining to do. Convince me to let you stay on, or Mort'll toss you out and let you walk. Without boots, you won't get too far in this heat."

"I feel good enough to do some work for you. Tend the horses, maybe do some carpentry. Looks as if the wagon needs it." Slocum saw cracks in the wagon's sides and had heard the creaking protest of rotting wood when Cara had entered earlier. "Don't know what else you'd need done. Don't rightly know what you do."

The woman leaned back and laughed. "Don't rightly know myself, sometimes. Mort Thorogoode's the owner of this show."

"A medicine show?"

"What else? Doctor Wong. That's really Mort, when he gets gussied up. And I'm Princess Lotus Blossom." Slocum had heard Thorogoode call her this back in the arroyo. "We mix up 'slum' and 'chopped grass' and sell it as one kind of medicine. Maybe do some 'flea powder' for another town."

Cara O'Connell saw the puzzled look on the man's face. She said, "You'll find out that we got a lingo all our own. Every medicine show does. Keeps us apart from the 'natives.'"

"The locals in the towns," Slocum guessed.

"You'll catch on just fine. Yes, the good citizens who buy our liquid medicines and herbs and powdered remedies."

"I don't know anything about selling," he told her.

"No need. Mort and I do the pitches. Billy and Frieda Ferguson do the crowd while we're pitching. No need for you to do anything except tend the horses and do some carpentry." Cara eyed Slocum critically. "But you don't look the type to be that good with a saw."

"I do what I have to."

"I'm sure you do, John." With a quick smile in his direction, Cara rose and moved with lithe grace to the back of the cramped wagon. She opened the door and swung out into the bright sunlight. Slocum struggled to sit up. While the bandages restricted his breathing and the stifling heat caused buckets of sweat to run down his body and begin to itch abominably, he tried standing. His strength returned quick enough to suit his purposes.

If Mort Thorogoode—Doctor Wong—travelled north to Albuquerque, that put the medicine show on the same route as Nathan and the others. Slocum felt coldness growing inside. Henry Nathan would pay for what he did. It was bad enough bushwhacking him like he'd done, but stealing his boots and pistol went too far. Nathan would pay. Dearly.

Slocum rummaged around in the racks covering the wagon walls until he found a few clear bottles sloshing half full with amber fluid. He uncorked one and took a deep sniff. He smiled. This was more like it. The vile-tasting "medicine" Cara had given him only caused his mouth to pucker. Slocum took a deep swallow of the whiskey he'd found and was rewarded with a burning heat that went all the way down his gullet and pooled nicely in his belly.

Settling onto the bunk again, he worked on the bottle until the only pain he knew was a memory. He never quite knew when he passed out.

"Billy's going to be powerful mad when he finds you drank all his whiskey," whispered Cara O'Connell.

"I knocked the bottom out of the bottle. Looks like it broke on its own and all the liquor dripped out."

"Billy gets real mean when he doesn't..." Cara bit back further words when the man came over and sat down heavily. The man's pale gray eyes bored into Slocum.

"You stayin' with us to Albuquerque?" Billy Ferguson asked without preamble.

"I asked him and he said yes," Cara cut in. "Slocum's a first-rate carpenter. You know how you been asking for a new stand? John can build you a nice one."

Billy looked skeptical. "I do a low pitch and need a box with a false bottom. Think you can build it for me?"

"I'll give it a try," Slocum promised. Billy grunted and left without another word.

"He works down among the natives," Cara explained. "He's the best damn clock man I ever saw. Steals watches sweet as you please, but he needs someplace to hide them." She turned and stared hard at Slocum. "That doesn't bother you, does it?"

"What?"

"That Billy swipes people's watches."

"Reckon there's worse things in the world to be than a pickpocket," Slocum allowed. Before Cara could say anything, Slocum went on, "Billy and Frieda are married?"

"You noticed. Yes, they fight like cats and dogs."

"Because of Billy's drinking?"

Cara looked at him even harder than before. She took several seconds before saying, "Yes, because of his drinking." Slocum knew she lied but didn't press the matter. He wasn't being totally honest with her. While everyone in Doctor Wong's Travelling Medicine Show looked to be a crook in some respect—selling fake patent medicines or picking men's pockets—Slocum didn't think they'd want to be tied in with his likes.

John Slocum, member of the notorious Nathan gang responsible for killing half a dozen innocent men and women in an ill-planned bank holdup. He snorted in disgust at himself. Even though he was stone broke, he should never have gone along with Nathan's hare-brained scheme. The man lacked any ability to engineer a real bank robbery. Slocum snorted in disgust again. While Nathan lacked talent for robbing banks, he didn't have any such lack when it came to double-crossing his partners. The bandages on Slocum's chest attested to that.

"Must have really been something," Cara said.

"What's that?"

"Somebody getting close enough to bushwhack you. You're a distant man, John Slocum. You carry around a lot of secrets."

"Is this part of the show? Mind reading?"

Cara nodded. "Mort and I've done a bit of that in our time. Fact is, that's how we got together. Mort was doing his brother John routine through Missouri a couple years back."

"He was peddling patent medicines as a priest?" The idea struck Slocum as ridiculous. He laughed when Cara nodded.

"Mort's good at it. You'd think it was the Lord God Almighty come to earth to give you the cure for what ails you when he swings into the pitch. Anyhow, Mort decided to change the pitch and do a mentalist act. I wanted away from Springfield so he took me on."

"I learned all the tricks. Mort'd say something and I'd take the first letter of the second word. That letter was a code for something, say a lady's handkerchief or a six-shooter. I'd struggle a mite, then announce it, even though I wore a thick blindfold. The natives never twigged to what we were doing."

Slocum nodded. He saw how the color returned to Cara's face as she recalled those days. Normally pale, even wan, the flush rising to her cheeks showed how animated she could get. For Cara, this was show business, and the lure of performing excited her. Slocum wondered what else got her all hot and bothered.

"There wasn't any way for me to just move on when we reached New Orleans. I stayed on with Mort and we worked up a new act."

"How long do you stay in each town?" Slocum didn't want Nathan and the others getting too far ahead of him. While they wouldn't be running as hard as if they knew he dogged their trail, they'd be wary of the law and wouldn't slow down for a considerable piece. Maybe they'd run to Santa Fe or cut over to Arizona Territory. If they did, he wanted to get after them as soon as possible.

"Not long. One or two shoes. We usually sell out everything we've got made up and then move on." Cara made a wry face. "Sometimes the law runs us out. That bother you?"

"You keep asking if going against the law worries me. Why don't you just come out and ask what's on your mind?"

"What's got you running from the law?" Cara asked bluntly.

Slocum settled back and looked around. Billy and Frieda worked over to one side of the camp, near the wagon. Of Mort Thorogoode he saw no trace. The campfire blazed merrily and kept away the desert's night chill. He'd finished off a can of beans and half a one of peaches and felt better than he had in weeks. The whiskey still held the pain down, and Cara O'Connell was a lovely woman.

Still, Slocum considered whether it was better to lie or tell the unvarnished truth. His trouble with the law dated way back to the final days of the War. He'd crossed Quantrill and Bloody Bill Anderson over the Lawrence, Kansas, raid and ended up shot. Took months to heal and by then Lee had surrendered at Appomattox Court-house. Slocum had thought his troubles were over.

They'd only begun.

A carpetbagger judge and a hired gun had taken a fancy to the land of Slocum's Stand in Calhoun County, Georgia. No taxes paid on the farm, the judge had said when he came with his hired gun to take it and turn that fine farmland into a stud ranch. By the end of the day, when John Slocum rode out, two new graves dotted the top of the ridge, and a price had been levied on his head for the killings.

No one liked judge killers, even carpetbagger judges during the Reconstruction. Slocum had kept moving and had survived somehow. Times had been good, times had been bad, but he had survived.

"If you're going to lie to me," Cara said, "it had better be a good one. I'm used to listening to Mort. He's about the best damned liar I ever heard. Make you think black is white while he's stealing your Union suit."

"No lie. There's enough lawmen around who'd consider it their duty to bring me to trial."

"In El Paso?"

"There. Back in Georgia, too."

"You do get around, John Slocum." Cara O'Connell dropped the subject and poked idly at the dying fire. Slocum rested, watching the dancing light playing over the fine planes and lines of the woman's face. Slocum figured she could sell sand to the Apaches. He couldn't think of any man who wouldn't be entranced with her beauty.

She turned and smiled almost shyly, as if reading his mind.

Cara started to speak, but Slocum jerked upright. "Don't move a muscle," he ordered. The snap in his voice froze her to the spot.

A rattler coiled behind Cara, its spade-shaped head darting this way and that. Slocum knew the signs. The poisonous snake was fixing to strike, and Cara O'Connell was its target.

3

"What's the matter?" Cara O'Connell asked, not looking the least bit upset.

Slocum moved like lightning. Fingers curled around a sharp rock, he stood and smashed the rock down on the rattler's head. The man jerked to one side as the snake struck—but it was at Slocum and not at Cara. This feeble effort on the snake's part meant its death.

Slocum smashed the rock down again as hard as he could on the snake's head. The tail moved feebly, the rattling noise barely audible over Cara's shrieks.

"What are you doing, John? My God, no, you killed it!"

"It was ready to strike," Slocum said, feeling a little faint. He sat down hard, his chest heaving and starting to hurt something fierce. "Got it in time, though."

"You killed it!" The woman stared in horror at the snake. "God, is Mort ever going to be angry at this!"

The woman's fingers stroked over the snake's battered spine and head just as they had over Slocum's wounds.

29

He looked at her in stark surprise. She wasn't afraid of the snake. If anything, she *liked* it.

Cara picked up the broken snake and held it. She turned to Slocum and said angrily, "It took a solid week of hunting to find one this docile and you killed it! How dare you!"

"It was coiled and ready to strike. It would have bit you." Slocum was getting angry now. He'd saved Cara from a savage and potentially deadly snake, and she had no call being like this with him. "Maybe I should have let it sink its fangs into you."

"What fangs?" Cara thrust the snake head out and fixed thumb and forefinger on either side of the snake's jaw. Squeezing forced open the mouth. "Do you see any fangs?"

"They fold back up into the snake's mouth," Slocum said. "That's why you can't see them."

"You can't see them because they've been removed. This rattler doesn't have any fangs. It can't hurt anyone."

Slocum frowned.

"Mort defanged it. We used it in our act. He puts on his Doctor Wong suit and lets it rattle and crawl all over him. It looks as if the snake bit him and gets a rise out of the natives. Then he takes a swig of his magical elixir and is all right again."

"There wasn't any way for me to know the snake was harmless." Slocum still wasn't convinced. He didn't go out of his way to kill rattlers, like some men he knew. The snakes served a good purpose, eating rodents and insects, but when they were coiled and rattling he wasn't going to take any chances. If he'd had a gun, he would have shot it. Even now, knowing what Cara had told him, he wouldn't do a thing different, given the same situation.

Some reactions were wrong and got a man killed. Others worked and kept him alive. Slocum hadn't survived this long making the wrong choices.

"He used it with the mongoose, too," Cara said, her voice lackluster now.

Slocum said nothing. For several minutes they sat in silence, listening to the distant howling of lovelorn coyotes and the fire popping and crackling. Cara jumped when Mort Thorogoode came blundering over. The man was drunk and barely stayed on his feet.

"Where's Milo?" Thorogoode said, words slurring. "Lost the damn snake. You seen him?"

Cara motioned for Slocum to stay silent as she shifted and hid the snake's body from view under her skirts. "No, Mort, I haven't seen him. You haven't let him get away, have you?"

"Cage was open. Billy musta cleaned it and forgot." Mort Thorogoode stared at Slocum with an expression bordering on pure hatred, then stumbled back into the darkness, grumbling about Billy letting his defanged snake loose.

"I would have told him," said Slocum. "There wasn't any need to cover for me."

"Wouldn't bring Milo back," the blonde said. "You heard what he said. Billy left the cage open. Can't expect wild animals to stay around, even with wild animals like us." She smiled and Slocum found himself returning it.

"Any other beasts I ought to know about? I'm likely to club anything out of the ordinary."

"We're low on animals right about now," Cara said. "The sidewinder Mort caught when he found you and Milo were the only snakes. There is a mongoose, but we can't use him."

"Mongoose?"

"Looks like a weasel. They use them in India for killing cobras."

"Don't need a mongoose for killing rattlers," Slocum said wryly, "when you have me and a rock."

Cara laughed at this. "It doesn't work that way. The

mongoose might be faster than a cobra, but we found out the hard way that rattlers are faster than a mongoose. Lost three of the four we started with learning that. Mort had some idea of using Milo and the mongoose in the show, but we couldn't figure out how to keep the mongoose from killing a harmless rattler."

"You folks work mighty hard thinking up new acts."

"That's what keeps us in money. We do well, we pitch hard, and we keep a sharp eye out for penny-weighters." When she saw Slocum's look of incomprehension, Cara explained. "Diamond thieves. Some of us in the travelling shows do well enough to buy diamonds. Portable wealth, and it impresses the high society matrons."

"But there are also those in the shows—the penny-weighters—who make a point of stealing your diamonds, is that it?"

"No honor among thieves."

Slocum's head swung in crazy circles. Clock men and pennyweighters and mongooses fighting defanged rattlers. He couldn't sort it all out right, especially not when his chest was hurting again. The numbing effects of the whiskey he'd drunk had begun to wear off.

"I'd best bunk down for the night. Not feeling all that strong yet."

"Go on, use the wagon one more night," Cara said. "It's a nice night, and I don't mind sleeping under the stars for a change. Be ready to move early in the morning, though. We're getting into Hot Springs before noon so we can set up for an evening show."

"The spare boots fit?" asked Thorogoode. He eyed Slocum critically. He shook his head in disgust at Slocum's appearance.

"Fine, thanks. A bit loose, but better than nothing." Slocum hammered away reinforcing the tailgate of the wagon. Some nails had popped loose and the planks had become uneven. While he wasn't the best carpenter in the world, he was obviously better than anyone with Doctor Wong's Travelling Medicine Show. Before they moved on to Hot Springs, Slocum had the tailgate reworked enough to use as a stage.

They rattled and clanked along the sun-baked, deeply rutted dirt road until they were less than a mile from Hot Springs. Thorogoode pulled over and came around to join Slocum and the Fergusons riding in the back of the wagon.

"Time to get ready," the man said. He opened trunks and took down vials from the racks along the wagon's sides. Slocum watched in quiet amusement as Thorogoode transformed himself into Doctor Wong, the wily Oriental capable of revealing all the secrets of the Ancient and Wondrous Celestial Empire to worthy citizens—for a price. Thorogoode's light brown hair got a quick rinse with a dark dye before being pulled back into a tight bun at his crown. Cara affixed a long artificial queue that fell midway down Thorogoode's spine. Tiny tucks were taken at the corners of his eyes and held in place with bits of plaster. Finishing it off was a lemon yellow paste that turned Thorogoode's natural pallor into a jaundice.

"Aren't you using too much?" asked Slocum. "You look sick, not Chinese."

Cara shushed him. "Don't upset Mort when he's getting ready for a pitch. And don't worry. The yokels don't know what a Chinaman looks like. Even if they do, Doctor Wong comes from another province, and that's the way they look there."

Cara O'Connell's transformation was equally startling. She pushed her blonde hair up and under a coarse black wig. The quilted black coat she put on dragged the floor and kept her from requiring more extensive makeup. A quick smear of Thorogoode's yellow paste turned her into a lighter version of Doctor Wong.

"From the same province," joked Slocum.

"Of course. We come, you betcha, from Fu King Province, velly velly far up north." Cara—Princess Lotus

Blossom—placed her hands together and bowed.

"First time I ever saw a green-eyed Chinese woman," said Slocum, still skeptical that this outrageous charade would work. He envisioned them all run out of town on a rail when the local sheriff decided that they were all frauds.

"Most solly," Cara said, "but am not pure Chinee. Mother Empress of all Chinee, father 'Mellican sailor who commanded her love. Tragic story."

"Do you make all that up as you go along, or is it all practiced?" he had to ask.

"Both. Never found a native yet, though, who thought up a new question. Ladle out the tragedy and they'll believe anything, especially if it sounds as if poor little Princess Lotus Blossom is worse off than they are."

"Cut the chatter," snapped Mort Thorogoode. "Time to perform." He quickly checked his Princess Lotus Blossom, nodded curtly, then gave Billy and Frieda Ferguson a once-over. They had changed into simpler clothing than they wore on the trail, but Slocum noticed that the tatters and rents hid pockets. "Hot Springs don't require permits, so we set up for this evening's performance and another tomorrow. By then, all that wants Doctor Wong's Virility Elixir and Restorer of Nerves will have bought, and we can move on."

"Got it all ready, Mort," spoke up Billy. The man pulled out a case of rattling bottles filled with a vile-looking yellow fluid. He began applying labels.

Mort left to get up front to drive. Cara flashed Slocum a quick smile and followed. While her husband worked on applying the labels to the phony elixirs, Frieda sat down on the bunk beside Slocum.

"You really fix Billy up with a false-bottomed pitch box?"

"Don't see why not. Drop something in the top and it falls on through to the hidden compartment. Maybe put in a catch so he can pick and choose what goes through."

THE JOURNEY OF DEATH 35

Frieda Ferguson looked at him with real admiration. "You in the business? You don't talk like us, but you sure do think like you been on the road."

Slocum denied being either a high or low pitchman. "How did Mort know Hot Springs didn't require any permits? You been through here before?"

"Never, but we talked with Silk Hat Harry in El Paso. Harry was passing through on his way to Dallas. Been working out in Arizona Territory and he'd hit Hot Springs about six months back. Farther north along the *Jornado del Muerte* is another matter. Heard rumors that they don't hold with any travelling shows."

"Sounds as if you are pretty friendly with other peddlers."

"We're all in the same business. Why not?" Frieda asked. "Call it Rattlesnake Oil or Doctor Wong's Magic Elixir for Warts and Catarrh. All the same."

The woman was considerably older than Cara. Slocum guessed she had lived with the travelling shows for a goodly portion of her life. Just how prosperous it had made her wasn't apparent while she was dressed in her working rags. From all that was said, a good pitchman made a considerable amount of money. Doctor Wong just didn't display it, but Slocum counted that as wise. It never paid to show your hand till all the cards were laid on the table.

"You going to work the natives or just watch?" Frieda Ferguson eyed Slocum with obvious intent. Her tongue poked through her lips and made a slow circuit in what she thought was a seductive move. Slocum glanced over at her husband. Billy licked the labels, occasionally took a swig from a whiskey bottle he'd found somewhere, and put the finishing touches on the bottles of elixir. He paid his wife no heed.

"Cara gave me a dollar, in addition to the boots, so I figure on finding a saloon and doing some serious drinking," Slocum said. This caught Billy's attention. "I'd only be in your way once you get going. I don't know anything about peddling snake oil."

"It is an art," Frieda allowed. "Now and then you see a native's face go blank. You lost 'em for sure. But when' their eyes get as round as saucers and their heads bob up and down like you got them on a string, there's nothing you can't sell them."

The wagon pulled to a halt. Slocum glanced out the back and saw that Thorogoode had stopped at the edge of Hot Springs. An undertaker's parlor was less than ten yards away, then a stable and general store.

"Help with the stage," ordered Thorogoode. He stood back and watched in silence. Slocum guessed that the inscrutable Doctor Wong couldn't be seen publicly performing such menial chores, but Slocum didn't mind. He secured the tailgate with a couple of rusty chains, made sure it was sturdy enough for Doctor Wong and Princess Lotus Blossom. Seeing that this was ready, Slocum tended the two mules, making sure they had water and a good patch of grass to graze on. Only then did he then stand back and watch the show.

Billy and Frieda began ringing bells and banging on kettles. At first, the crowd was slow to form. Slocum wondered how long it would be before Doctor Wong began his pitch. He simply stood with hands hidden in voluminous sleeves, staring out over Hot Springs. Princess Lotus Blossom knelt at his feet, head bowed. They held this tableau for almost fifteen minutes. Just as those who'd come started to mumble and drift away, Doctor Wong threw his arms into the air and shouted, "You all die! You all die slowly!"

And then he got into his pitch about the evils of modern living, how the ancients hid their most valuable knowledge and only he, Doctor Wong from the Celestial Empire, dared reveal these secrets. Slocum was amused that Doctor Wong stopped just short of naming a price. He skillfully shifted attention to Princess Lotus Blossom, who had remained kneeling until now. She rose and began a slow, not too graceful dance—the forbidden "Ritualistic Mating Dance of the Mongol Hordes," Doctor Wong explained.

Frieda Ferguson played the instruments, Princess Lotus Blossom danced, and Doctor Wong sized up the crowd. All the while, Billy Ferguson moved through the assembled knot of citizens, offering a dozen different trinkets for sale. Slocum watched closely and finally decided this was only a way for Billy to find out how much money each had—and where it was kept. Hip pockets, coat pockets, those were the easy pickings for him. At least two watches vanished into the hidden recesses of Billy's ragged coat. Slocum wondered at the wisdom of stealing like this when the crowd was more than willing to pay for all the secrets of China, but he didn't let it worry him too much. He recognized professionals. Those in Doctor Wong's Travelling Medicine Show were skilled at what they did, and he was only a rank amateur.

Princess Lotus Blossom stopped her dance and Doctor Wong picked up smoothly, extolling the virtues of living to be one hundred and twenty-three years old, as he was. Slocum drifted to the edge of the growing crowd and headed into the heart of Hot Springs. The dollar Cara had given him wasn't enough to purchase a new pistol, but it would provide a few good drinks and maybe a bottle of cheap whiskey to take along when they left town.

The Loco Weed Saloon had less than a dozen patrons bellied up to the bar and none at all sitting around the card tables. Slocum guessed the usual crowd had gone out to see Doctor Wong's Travelling Medicine Show. The noise and crush of a saloon wasn't what he sought, though.

"Anything but trade whiskey," he told the barkeep. The expression on the man's face told him he was out of luck. Either he forced down the mixture of alcohol, black powder, and chewing tobacco or he drank nothing.

Slocum sighed and nodded, dropping a dime on the bar.
He got a shot of the trade whiskey.

"Haven't seen you around before. You just passin'
through?" asked the man next to him at the bar.

Before Slocum could tell the man it was none of his
business, the man turned and showed a shiny badge pinned
to his shirt front.

"Just passing through." Slocum didn't say any more.
He'd found out a long time back that it was safer to let
the sheriff do the asking. Whatever information was volunteered, it was always taken wrong.

"With the medicine show?"

"Handyman. Drive a few nails, clean the tack, menial
stuff."

The sheriff's eyes worked from the top of Slocum's
head to his ill-fitting boots. He itched to say something
about how Slocum looked to be a man used to carrying
a gun, but he finished his drink instead.

"Best go hear the show," the sheriff said. He left
without a backward look. Slocum rested easier. He bought
a half-bottle of the cheap whiskey for fifty cents and took
it and a clean glass to a table in the back of the saloon. The
past few days had been more than he wanted to live through
again. Shotgunned, left for dead, scared half to death by
a defanged rattler, working for a man who dressed himself
up as a Chinaman—Slocum had been through better times.

But the thought of Henry Nathan turned him to ice
inside. No man did what Nathan had done and lived to
brag on it. And Slocum had Nathan pegged well. The
man would be shooting his mouth off to anyone who'd
listen. It was bad enough he had advertised to all of El
Paso del Norte who had robbed their bank. If Nathan
thought any shred of notoriety went along with it, he'd
be boasting how he had killed John Slocum.

Slocum knocked back another glass of the coarse,
burning whiskey. It didn't settle him. It made him even
madder. It might take a while, but he would catch up

with Nathan and make him pay. There was so much more to this than the money from the robbery. Slocum's honor had been sullied. And he was *mad*.

Heavy, uneven footsteps echoed through the mostly empty saloon as a man entered from the direction of the back rooms. Slocum had seen the doorway and figured it went to the cribs. In a town this size, not more than two or three whores would be working regular. He didn't even bother turning around to look at the sated patron.

Lost in his own thoughts, Slocum drank in silence until the man who'd been with the whore shouted at the bartender, "Cheap shit! What do you mean giving a man like me this cheap shit!" A bottle smashed against a wall, sending glass flying.

Slocum turned and stared at the man's back. At first he didn't recognize him—his eyes fixed on the ebony handles of the two Colt Navys slung in a crossdraw holster.

His holster. His Colts.

Slocum half rose when the man at the bar whipped out one of the Colts and cocked it. He pointed it directly at the bartender's head. Slocum sank back down in his chair to wait. It was bad enough being unarmed and going up against a man sporting two pistols. Slocum didn't feel suicidal enough to approach anyone with a gun already drawn and cocked.

"I want the good stuff."

"Yes, sir," the barkeep said, only the throbbing of a big blue vein in his forehead betraying his nervousness.

He sat the bottle in front of Walt Larouche. Slocum couldn't help smiling when he saw it was from the same case that the prior bottle had come from. He almost laughed when Larouche pronounced this to be vastly better swill.

But Larouche didn't holster the black-handled Colt. He left it on the bar close at hand. Slocum considered walking over and smashing the whiskey bottle over Larouche's head, then discarded the idea. He wouldn't get halfway there before the man heard him. As keyed up as Larouche seemed, he might start shooting at any instant, for no reason at all.

"Know who I am?" Larouche demanded of the barkeep.

"Can't rightly say I do, but you must be somebody important."

"Damn right I am! I'm Walt Larouche of the Nathan gang. We held up every bank between here'n El Paso del Norte. What do you think of that?"

"Don't think one way or the other. All I do's sell whiskey." The barkeep's face twitched a bit more now when he saw that Larouche was both drunk and crazy. "Makes you real important, I guess."

"Damn important. 'Bout the most important outlaw in New Mexico Territory. Real *desperado*."

Slocum got to his feet and slipped out the back way. If he stayed much longer, Larouche would eventually turn and spot him. Then all hell would break loose. On the other hand, if Slocum sat quietly outside the saloon and waited, Larouche would eventually come stumbling out. When he did, he would pay for stealing those Colt Navys. The guns were Slocum's pride and joy, carefully tended, the gunsmithing done on them personally. While he didn't like the idea of Larouche having them for one second longer than necessary, Slocum knew when to sit and wait.

He found a wooden chair in front of the Loco Weed Saloon, rocked back in it, and waited for Larouche to leave.

In less than an hour a commotion started in the saloon. A couple of shots broke glass and someone—the barkeep?—swore a blue streak. Larouche stumbled out into the dusty street, cocked gun in hand, waving it around wildly. Slocum tipped himself forward and sat in the shadows, his heart racing faster. His hands itched to be wrapped around Larouche's throat.

And after he throttled Nathan's whereabouts out of Larouche, he would just keep tightening his grip until the murderous Larouche was no more. It was certainly a better fate than the man deserved. He might not have pulled the trigger on Slocum, but he bragged on it. That might count as even worse in Slocum's mind.

Slocum got to his feet and quietly stalked Larouche down the quiet streets of Hot Springs. Sulphur fumes from the mineral baths made his nose wrinkle, and the darkness caused Larouche to pop in and out of sight, but Slocum had found his target. He wouldn't miss.

Quickening his pace, he overtook Larouche. One hand on the man's shoulder spun him around. The other hand tightened into a fist and shot out. Slocum had no desire to break bones. His punch went straight for Larouche's belly. Slocum swung so hard he buried his fist wrist-deep in the soft flesh.

Larouche's arms shot out, and he looked like a bow without either string or arrow for a moment. He staggered back and sat down heavily on the wooden sidewalk.

"Good evening," Slocum said in a conversational tone. "You must be the outlaw all the lawmen are looking for."

"N-no, please, no," gasped out Larouche. "You got the wrong man. Not me."

"But you're Walt Larouche, aren't you," Slocum said, taking a fiendish pleasure in tormenting the man. "Killed a dozen women and children, robbed banks, stole horses. Can't decide whether to turn you over to a lynch mob or let you live to stand trial."

"Please, mister, I got money. It's yours if..." Larouche recovered enough to see his tormentor. "God, no! You're dead. Henry left you for dead."

"He's as lousy a shot as you are a bank robber," Slocum snapped. He stepped up and kicked Larouche in the side when the man fumbled for the Colt at his left side. Slocum retrieved his pistols. After strapping them around his waist, he felt better than he had in days.

"The boots," he said. "Take them off." Larouche

moaned constantly as he worked to get Slocum's boots off.

"They forced me to take these. Henry and Nails. They made me take your boots. Honest, Slocum. I didn't want to, but they made me."

Slocum thought of putting a single bullet in Larouche's head, then decided not to bother. It was like killing a cockroach. A distasteful chore, but it didn't gain anyone anything. There was always another to take its place.

"Where's Nathan? I got a score to settle with him."

"Henry? God, Slocum, he'd kill me if I told."

"I'll kill you if you don't."

The cold, matter-of-fact tone made Larouche start to shake.

"It was all his idea. I wanted to split the money with you. Honest, I did, but Henry, he wanted more."

"Where is Nathan?"

The shot tore at Slocum's left bicep but it didn't draw blood—the shot wasn't aimed at him. It found a messy target in the center of Larouche's forehead. In the dark, at the distance from which it had come, this could only be called a lucky shot. Slocum didn't believe Nathan or any other man was a good enough shot to have killed like this otherwise. But luck didn't matter one whit to Walt Larouche any more. He was dead.

Slocum turned and looked out across the deserted street. No one in Hot Springs stirred. They were all out at Doctor Wong's Travelling Medicine Show being sold bottles of fake elixir for diseases they didn't have.

All except for one. He figured that had to be Henry Nathan.

John Slocum slipped back in the shadows and went hunting.

4

Slocum judged angles and decided that the shot that killed Walt Larouche had been fired from the alley across the street. If the unseen sniper had been on the roof of the building, the porch roof would have protected Larouche. As it was, the only clear line of sight had to be that shadowy alley.

Slocum was going to convince whoever fired—probably Henry Nathan—that he had gone and backshot the wrong one. Larouche was relatively harmless. Slocum wasn't.

It felt good being back in his own boots and having his pistols weighing him down again. His thumb rubbed over the hammer of the Colt Navy in his hand. While Larouche hadn't taken particularly good care of the gun, neither had he gone out of his way to abuse it in the short time it had hung at his hip.

Slocum circled the Loco Weed Saloon and hurried across the street a few stores down. No shot rang out, no lead sought his flesh. He ducked further behind a large building holding the bank and two smaller stores, found another good-sized street, and made his way down to where the dingy alley opened. If the sniper hadn't moved, Slocum had circled behind and had him.

He entered cautiously, trying not to jump at every small noise. A mangy black tomcat prowled after a mouse. Wind whipping down the street and entering the alley set up a mournful whistling through loose planking in the building walls. For Slocum, the worst part was the inky darkness. Seeing anything more than vague outlines proved impossible.

A sound. Movement. A silhouette in the mouth of the alley against the lights from the Loco Weed Saloon. In a smooth motion, the Colt came up and the hammer went back. The click of the cocking hammer, slight though it was, alerted the figure.

"John?" came a familiar voice. "Is that you?"

Suspicious, Slocum slipped down the alley. He didn't lower the hammer until he was sure it was Cara O'Connell in front of him.

"What are you doing in this alley?" he asked.

"Might ask you the same, except I saw what happened." The woman gestured that they ought to walk. Her steps took them back toward Doctor Wong's Travelling Medicine Show.

"You saw who gunned down Larouche?"

"If that's his name. A man with a scarred-up face stood in the alley. One shot from a Remington. Here's the spent cartridge." She tossed Slocum a brass cylinder. He snorted and tossed it into a watering trough. No need to keep it.

"What were you doing wandering around Hot Springs? Thought you were doing your Princess Lotus Blossom act."

"Things close up quick in a small town like this. Mort made his pitch, we sold about fifty bottles of the elixir, and he decided to pack up so we could move on in the morning."

"No second show?" Slocum's eyes darted left and right, searching for some sign of Nathan. The man was nowhere to be seen.

"Not enough potential. Mort's good at sizing up a crowd. Thinks we done all we could today. He's muttering about changing the act, that the Doctor Wong routine is too much like others that have been through here in the past year."

"You didn't know the galoot doing the shooting back there?"

"Look here, John Slocum, I came looking for you and I see you beating up a man who gets shot down like a dog. What's going on? What are you mixed up in? We might find ourselves in a spot of trouble over not paying off the local law or having a forged work permit, but nobody gets killed. If you're being chased, you might as well find yourself another ride north."

"I'm not being chased," Slocum said grimly. "I'm doing the chasing."

"Well?" she said after it became apparent Slocum wasn't going to say any more. "Are you going to tell me about it?"

"No need worrying you."

"Let me decide, damn you!"

Slocum looked at Cara out of the corner of his eye. She was a feisty one, he had to admit. He'd seen women not half as pretty who thought they were high society and they ought to faint at the sight of a snake or go into a swoon whenever the mere mention of gunfighting came up. Not Cara O'Connell. She had lived out in a world populated by fake characters, changing her own to suit the crowds. An actress, but without a script or much of a cast or stage.

"It doesn't concern you."

"Does it have to do with how you ended up shotgunned and left for the buzzards?"

Slocum nodded curtly.

"Thought so." Cara moved closer and took Slocum's

arm. He started to pull away. If Nathan found them, Cara
might get in the way of a bullet. But the strength of her
grip on his arm kept him from easily dislodging her
without making a scene. Besides, if Nathan had an ounce
of good sense, he'd already be on his horse and riding
like the devil nipped at his heels.

Before Slocum was finished with him, he'd pray for
the devil to take him. The fate would be kinder.

"Just as well we're moving on right away. I doubt the
sheriff would like the looks of having a dead man on his
street."

"Were you and the man shot down friends? No," she
said quickly. "You wouldn't have struck him like that if
you'd been friends. He was drunk and you knocked him
down." Her green eyes dropped to take in the boots and
gun holstered at Slocum's side. The second Colt Navy
had been securely tucked into the belt. "He was the one
who bushwhacked you," she decided.

"Not him."

"Another. Another shot you and just missed killing
you again tonight."

"I suspect Nathan's done just what he intended, stupid
as it is. He got rid of Larouche and can tell Rawlinson
I did it."

"Nathan?" the woman asked. "I heard that name somewhere."

Slocum sighed. Henry Nathan's loud mouth had spread
the name more than anyone realized. For someone who
had done so damn little, he had built up a mighty big
reputation. Slocum tried to figure out how much to tell
Cara. Tell her too much and she might mention it to Mort
Thorogoode. Slocum didn't trust the owner of Doctor
Wong's Travelling Medicine Show one little bit. That
man would sell his own grandmother if the price was
right. On the other hand, if he told Cara nothing, her
agile mind would build up stories that might far exceed
reality. In the long run, this would be worse than telling
her everything.

"What happened, John?" Cara almost cooed. She snuggled closer, her lush body rubbing against his harder, muscled one. "I won't tell anyone. I promise."

"Not even Mort?"

He felt her stiffen and move away slightly. The reaction to his question surprised him. Maybe things weren't too good between Cara and the medicine show owner.

"Mort's got his ways," Cara said carefully, choosing her words with precision. "I'm getting around to not liking those ways too much any more."

"He beat you?"

"Nothing like that. No man could do that to me and not find a knife slipped between his ribs one night. Mort's got vices. Bad ones. You've seen how he gets."

Slocum frowned. He'd seen Thorogoode drunker than a skunk, but it had looked to be Billy Ferguson finding more solace in a bottle than a woman. If anyone complained, Slocum figured it ought to be Frieda Ferguson. But he decided Cara meant something more than just whiskey.

"You can leave him whenever you want," Slocum said.

"It's not that easy. Not for a woman. We make good money selling Doctor Wong's potions. I got a fair number of diamonds, and Mort's got a dress coat with twenty-dollar gold pieces for buttons. The coat cost him close to five hundred dollars to have tailor made in San Francisco."

"If you have the money . . ." Slocum's voice petered out.

"I said it wasn't that easy for a woman," Cara repeated. "Where would I go? There's money, but I've come to appreciate the finer things whenever we reach the big cities. I could never settle down in a jerkwater town like this. Hell, John, I can't even remember the name of this place! They all look the same to me."

Slocum still didn't see what she was getting at, but he figured it would come out soon enough. While he didn't like it, he knew Cara's plans included him. Disappointing her would be hard to do, but there wasn't any place for her if he was going to track down Henry Nathan and the burly Nails Rawlinson and pay them back for what they'd done to him.

The cut of the bank money had increased, too. With Larouche gone, that meant one fewer hand to spend those greenbacks.

"I got some money, but I'd need more. And I'd need someone to look after me."

"You seem to be doing a good enough job on that account," said Slocum. He found himself distracted now between Cara O'Connell and the crowd milling at the edge of Hot Springs. They'd walked the length of the main street and were within a few hundred yards of the medicine wagon. What attracted the most attention seemed to be Mort, still in his Doctor Wong getup, arguing with the sheriff.

"That's the kind of thing I mean, John," Cara said softly. She took his arm and steered him away until they stood in the shadows cast by the undertaker's parlour. "Mort's good at handling the local law. I could never do it. Not the way he does."

"If you gave up the show, you wouldn't have to."

"What! Give up my life? Whatever are you saying, John Slocum? I was talking about leaving Mort Thorogoode, not the medicine shows. They're my life, my very life!"

Slocum was startled at her outburst. He'd thought she worked her way around to telling him how she wanted to settle down in a big city and go to the opera and do society things. Instead, she twisted it around, declaring her intent to leave Thorogoode but keep on doing the travelling shows. Slocum had heard the stage lured some people, that they were less than alive when they weren't the center of attention with an audience dutifully appreciating their talents.

In a way, he understood. When he sat astride a good

spotted Nez Percé pony and looked down from the heights of the Wasatch Mountains, a feeling of power came to him. Not power over people, but over Nature, of sharing *with* Nature. Without having the words for it, he knew he belonged, that he formed a part of a larger picture. Take him out of the mountains and range country and put him in some city-fied coat and vest and cravat with a large diamond stickpin and he'd die. Just like a melon whose vine has been nicked, he'd begin to wither and dry up. Eventually he'd be only a husk of the man he'd been.

He needed the freedom of the mountains and plains, he needed to roam without jostling elbows with a hundred other folks. He needed all that as much as Cara O'Connell needed to be on stage performing.

"You make better money doing medicine shows than you would in San Francisco in a play?"

The expression on her face told him everything. Cara O'Connell might make more from the medicine shows than he could robbing banks. Hell, he'd heard it said that Jesse James never made more'n four or five thousand dollars total off his robbing. He wasn't anywhere near as intent on bank robbery as Jesse, nor did he want to be. That bank in El Paso del Norte had just been a temptation he should have passed on.

His fingers tensed around the butt of his gun as he thought once more of Nathan. Cara was safe enough now. He ought to go hunting for his one-time partner and settle the score once and for all time.

"John, I think Mort's being thrown in jail. Do something!"

The sheriff had gripped Doctor Wong by the elbow and lifted enough to get the man onto his toes. In this position it was easier to steer him toward the center of town and the jail. Thorogoode protested loudly in his fake pidgin English, maintaining his Chinese impersonation flawlessly.

"What's he suppose to have done?" asked Slocum.

"Who knows? No permit, someone didn't believe in the potion—it can be anything. You've got to help him."

"Might be a good chance to leave Thorogoode," Slocum pointed out. "With him in jail, you can leave with the show."

"I'll pretend I didn't hear you say that. That'd be stealing. This is *Mort's* show."

Slocum didn't try to figure the woman out. Cara saw nothing wrong in selling worthless or even dangerous elixirs to the people in the small towns, but robbing Mort of the show was worse than bushwhacking for her.

"How long's he likely to be locked up for if we don't do something?" Slocum wasn't going to tangle with the sheriff, not when the man hadn't yet discovered Larouche's corpse littering his clean street. Slocum hadn't forgot the going-over the sheriff had given him back in the Loco Weed Saloon, either. The sheriff had seen the look that set Slocum apart. There were only two kinds of people: predators and prey.

Slocum had the look of the hunter about him. No amount of acting could erase it, whether or not he wore a gun.

As the sheriff and Doctor Wong passed by, Slocum heard the sheriff saying, ". . . fake potions." That was all the clue he needed to know what had to be done.

He sucked in a chestful of air, winced at the pain it caused, and didn't have to act much when he let out a bellow of agony that rattled windows throughout the town. The sheriff swung around in time to see Slocum fall face forward into the dirt.

"What'n hell's the matter with him?" the sheriff demanded of Cara, who knelt over Slocum. Slocum kicked and moaned loudly, stirring up a small dust cloud to further hide his identity from the sheriff. It wouldn't do being seen with guns now when he hadn't worn them earlier.

"I've never seen him like this. Oh, my, Sheriff, I just

don't know what's wrong with him!" cried Cara. "Get a doctor. Find someone who can save his life!"

Thorogoode took his cue perfectly. He jerked free of the grip on his arm and straightened his black quilted robe. "I doctor. I fixee chop chop with Doctor Wong's Miracle Tonic."

"You'll only push him over the edge with that stuff," muttered the sheriff, trying to pull Doctor Wong back. But the fake Chinaman wasn't to be so easily deterred. He pulled forth a bottle filled with brown liquid and jerked out the cork with a flourish.

"Drinkee this and you be all light chop chop. You see."

Cara turned Slocum's head at an unnatural angle so she could pour the vile brown concoction into his mouth. Slocum didn't have to put on an act when he sputtered and shouted in protest.

"He's saved. Oh, Doctor Wong, you've saved him. How can I thank you!" Cara flung her arms around Thorogoode's neck and crushed herself to him.

"All in day's work. No need thankee Doctor Wong. Thank magic potion from Celestial Kingdom."

"I . . . I feel better," Slocum said, pulling himself to hands and knees. "It's a miracle. I never felt this good before." He stopped himself from saying anything more. To have done so would have made the sheriff suspicious. As it was, the few people remaining from the crowd watching Doctor Wong's show had gathered about. The buzz of conversation told Slocum that they believed now. Those dollar bottles of Doctor Wong's Magic Elixir would cure anything from warts to dropsy. And who knows, Slocum decided, if they believed hard enough it might actually work for them.

"Are you buying some of this miraculous potion, too, Sheriff?" asked Cara in her most ingenuous voice. Slocum marvelled that she dared openly face the sheriff after appearing on stage in her Princess Lotus Blossom costume. Even though she had changed clothes and had wiped off the thick yellow dye she'd worn, Slocum didn't see how the man could fail to recognize her.

He knew they'd all be thrown in the Hot Springs jail. But it didn't happen.

"I ... uh ... nothing of the sort," said the sheriff. "I just wanted to discuss a private matter with Doctor Wong. Come along, sir, so we can finish our business." This time, Slocum saw, the sheriff didn't drag Doctor Wong along. They walked together, but not as prisoner and lawman.

"You were marvelous, John," Cara crowed as soon as the sheriff and Thorogoode had vanished from sight. "We ought to put this into the show. We've used similar things but none's been this effective."

"Is the sheriff going to put Mort in jail?"

"Not now. He wouldn't dare. Too many of the natives saw the miracle cure." She laughed heartily. "Mort'll take about an hour to sell the sheriff a bottle or two of the elixir. Might end up telling him it'll cure the clap, too. The sheriff looks like the sort who'd worry about that."

Slocum got to his feet and brushed off the dirt. When Cara didn't say anything, he looked over at her. The expression on her face was unreadable.

"Come on into the wagon," she said softly. "We'll get cleaned up."

Her grip on his arm was even harder than before. He helped her up into the wagon and then followed. Barely had he pulled the door shut behind them when Cara spun around and flung her arms around his neck. The kiss she gave was more than a thank-you kiss. It unleashed floods of passion.

Slocum broke off and gasped for air. "Is this what you want?" he asked.

"Damn it, yes!" Cara O'Connell gave him no time to say anything more. Her mouth devoured his. At first Slocum was hesitant. Then he didn't even try to hold back. She was a vibrantly alive, sensuous woman—and she wanted him.

He wanted her.

His fingers worked at the catches on her dress. He got the top open to expose the sweet white melons of her breasts. Slocum couldn't have stopped now if all the Chinese in the world had come crashing through the door. His face lowered so he could kiss and suck and lick and tongue those wondrous breasts. Cara moaned softly, her fingers stroking through his raven-black hair. She thrust her chest out slightly to encourage him to do even more.

He did.

As he licked small wet circles on the tips of her breasts, enticing the coral buttons to full hardness, his hands lifted her skirts.

"Oh, yes, John. Now. Don't try to undress me all the way. I need you so. I have ever since I saw you."

"You're a beautiful woman, Cara."

"And this is going to be mine!" Slocum grunted as Cara got his gunbelt free and let it fall to the floor. Her long fingers unbuttoned his trousers and found the hard length straining behind the tough denim. He grunted again as she began stroking up and down.

Together they sank to the floor. Her long skirts hiked up to expose bare legs and the most delicious sight Slocum could remember. Her legs on either side of his waist, he slipped his hands under her buttocks and lifted her off the wagon floor. The carnal target beckoned to him.

"I don't want it gentle. Give it to me as hard as you can. Hurry, John, hurry, my darling. Now, do it now!"

They both gasped when Slocum sank deep into her clutching interior. For a long moment, he held himself upright on his straight arms, hips thrust forward, eyes closed, doing nothing but savoring the sensations pouring into his body.

"So nice," he muttered. "Never been this good before."

"Make it even better," she urged. Slocum didn't have

to be told twice. He bent forward until his weight crushed Cara to the hard floor. Her breasts compressed and the hard nipples poked fervently at his chest. Small pain twinges went through him; he still wasn't recovered from the shotgun blast. But the pleasure outdistanced the pain.

With hands cupping her well-rounded rear, he lifted and sank even farther into her moist inner reaches. Slocum felt Cara's lithe, strong legs locking around his. Her ankles pressed against the insides of his thighs so she could lift herself up and drive his erection still deeper into her needy body.

She began to whimper and moan in joy as he slid out till only the tip of his manhood remained inside her. Then he stroked powerfully. It lifted her off the floor again. Cara gasped and moaned and began thrashing about as the tempo of their actions joined and began to work for their common pleasure.

Her hips ground in passionate little circles. Slocum drove hard and fast, straight up the middle. Wet sucking noises of their coupling filled the wagon, only to be drowned out by Cara's gasps of stark carnal pleasure.

"Yes, oh, so close, so close."

"You want more of this," he teased, lifting her ass and slipping forward very slowly. He tormented her with every single inch until she let out a gasp and tensed. Her body began to flutter like a leaf in a high wind.

And Slocum grunted as he felt her body surround his hidden length. She clamped down on him like a mineshaft collapsing. Slocum couldn't keep up the smooth, even motion now. His own desires had been enflamed by the woman's demanding body. Going all out, his every motion designed to heighten both their enjoyment, he erupted in a surge of intense soul-searing joy.

Arms locked around each other, they lay side by side on the narrow floor, spent.

"I knew it," Cara said softly.

"What's that?"

"I knew you were something special the first time I laid eyes on you, John Slocum."

"Wasn't so special then. I was more dead than alive."

Cara laughed as she reached between their sweaty bodies and found what she sought. "You feel more dead than alive now, too. Are you always like this, John?"

He soon proved to her that he wasn't.

5

With Cara peacefully sleeping, a smile curling the corners of her lips, Slocum rose from the narrow bunk and swung free. The wood planking under his feet protested, but the sound wasn't loud enough to wake the sleeping woman. Slocum stared down at her for a minute, thinking how lovely she was. Her hair looked like spun gold, drifting gently over one eye. If an angel had come to Earth and taken human form, she couldn't have been lovelier.

But Cara O'Connell was no angel when it came to her lovemaking. She was a devil, voraciously taking all Slocum could give and wantonly asking for more. He wouldn't have wanted it any other way.

Slocum picked up his boots and gunbelt and went outside the wagon. The night had turned cold, as it did in the desert. He put on his boots and strapped his gunbelt tightly around his waist. He had a man to find. Somewhere in Hot Springs, Henry Nathan waited for him.

Starting into town, Slocum ran into Mort Thorogoode. Thorogoode's Doctor Wong outfit looked the worse for

wear and the man staggered heavily. Slocum caught him
before he toppled onto his face.

"What happened?" Slocum demanded, thoughts of the
sheriff beating Thorogoode running through his mind.
Propping up the phony Doctor Wong convinced Slocum,
however, that he hadn't been beaten. And no stench of
spilled liquor came to assault Slocum's nostrils. Whatever had happened to Thorogoode, it had been devas-
tating and left no outward signs.

"Nothing happened. Get me back to the wagon."
Thorogoode held onto Slocum until they reached the back
of the medicine wagon. Then Thorogoode straightened
his shoulders and seemed to pull himself together. He
climbed onto the tiny stage and entered the wagon.Slocum
considered following him in, then decided against it.
Whatever went on between Thorogoode and Cara was
their business. Slocum was an interloper, and the medicine show had existed well before his arrival and would
continue doing well after he left.

Slocum retraced his steps and found Hot Springs packed
up for the night. All the stores had long since closed and
nary a light burned. The heavy sulphur smell from the
mineral baths drew him. He figured that a braggart like
Nathan would stay at only the finest of hotels. After all,
he had plenty of money. Why not spend it on good
accommodations? A nickel-a-night flophouse wouldn't
do for the most wanted outlaw this side of the Rio Grande.

The Hot Springs Hotel stood on a low hill and was
obviously a finer place to stay than the hotel on the town's
main street. Slocum didn't bother going to find the clerk.
The stables were the best spot to begin his search.

Slipping into the barn, he heard loud snoring from the
rear. Trying not to spook any of the horses, he walked
down the middle and peered into each stall. He found
his horse—no doubt taken by Walt Larouche, who had
also acquired his pistols and boots—and another he
thought he remembered as being one tied up in the arroyo

where he'd been shot, but of Nathan's horse he found no trace.

"What you wantin', mister? We're all closed down for the night," came a low voice. A young stablehand rubbed the sleep from his eyes and yawned widely. "See me in the morning if'n you want your horse."

"Wanted to pick up my friend's horse. Horses. Those two."

"Them?" The tow-headed boy yawned again, then scratched his head. "Not my place to say so, but tell your friend he's been mistreatin' those animals something fierce."

"How's that?"

"Dirty, not curried for a week or more, hungry. Least you can do is let a horse graze a mite. Not much out on the road this time of year, but there's enough if you give the horse time to find it."

"How much is the bill?"

"Don't rightly know. Jeb, up at the front desk, he takes care of money."

"Think this might put it right with you if I took the horses now?" Slocum flipped a silver dime to the boy, who deftly caught it.

"Think I'd rather let the owner take 'em himself."

Another dime. The boy's resolve weakened. Slocum hoped it would break soon. All he had left was twenty cents. A third dime convinced the fellow to let the horses go.

"Must be something powerful exciting happening out there tonight," the boy said, as he got the horses' tack.

"Why's that?"

"Your other friends rode out of here 'bout two hours ago like their shirttails were on fire."

"You mean a man with a scarred face and another gent, about as big as a house."

"Them's the ones. The big guy musta been a smithy at one time. You can tell from the wrists and forearms.

Strong. And he knew how to tend horses, too. Not like the owner of these."

"You've done a good job. Much obliged. And I'll see to it that they're given better care."

The boy grumbled a little and then returned to the storeroom where he had a bunk. Slocum led the horses out, not bothering to ride. With Nathan and Rawlinson already on the trail for two hours, he'd not have much chance of finding them. If they turned back on the trail and went toward El Paso, he'd never find them. The ground had been baked until it was harder than a painted Mexican clay pot. Slocum's only hope of tracking down the pair lay in them going north, toward New Albuquerque and Santa Fe.

He thought about riding on after them, but with only twenty cents in his pocket he wouldn't get far. No food, not enough money to buy bullets and powder; he was handicapped even if he could overtake them.

With no real sense of reluctance, Slocum returned to Doctor Wong's Travelling Medicine Show. A few more days with the show wouldn't be too bad, he told himself. If Thorogoode kept his distance and Cara didn't, those days might be damned good.

Slocum learned why the Spanish called this the *Jornado del Muerte*—the journey of death. The summer sun beat down harder than any he'd ever experienced. The mules pulling the medicine wagon grew weaker and weaker, in spite of frequent rest stops. Slocum had asked Thorogoode why they didn't wait until evening to travel, but the man had grunted and brushed off the question.

Slocum had seen a new side to Thorogoode in that instant. The man's complexion had turned deathly pale, his eyes were mere pits in his head, and a wildness about him changed him into something closer to animal than human. At first Slocum thought it was being out in the harsh desert. Then he remembered how Thorogoode had looked when he was stumbling back to the wagon the previous night.

"It's one of the reasons I want to get away," Cara said softly. She seemed to be able to read his mind at moments like this. Slocum pulled his attention away.

"What makes him like this?"

"He's too damned cussed to be any other way," she said. The answer told Slocum nothing. Whatever was making Thorogoode like this, it wasn't natural. He'd seen men drunk and Thorogoode hadn't been liquored up the night before. He'd seen men hung over, and Thorogoode wasn't in that sorry state.

"He's making a big mistake tackling the desert in midday. The mules might not make it. Hell, the horses are just tethered to the wagon and not carrying any weight, and I don't know if they'll make it." Slocum glanced out the wagon's opened back door at the two horses trotting along. Foam slathered their sides and they both looked closer to dead than alive.

"Mort doesn't notice."

"He was sweating like a pig," Slocum said.

Cara only shrugged and glanced over to where Billy and Frieda Ferguson sat. Frieda idly worked through a deck of fortune-telling cards, not paying much attention to them as they slid around on the floor. Billy snored loudly, sleeping off his drunk. He had worked the Hot Springs crowd well and had garnered half a dozen pocket watches and almost fifty dollars in greenbacks. How much of that he had used to buy whiskey Slocum didn't know, but from the rattle and clink of hidden bottles, he guessed it had been a goodly portion.

"Don't worry about Billy," said Cara. "We can always use the extra bottles. Doctor Wong actually has to buy empties now and again for his potion."

"What goes into that?" Slocum pointed to a bottle filled with the vile liquid Thorogoode had used to "restore" him to health.

"I throw in a variety of things. Oil of capsicum..."

"What's that?" asked Slocum.

"Red pepper. It's used in liniments and the like. Cape aloe makes the liquid bitter and acts as a physic, might put in some cascara bark or sugar, and if I can get a good supply, aniseed or berberis root from Europe."

"Does any of that *do* anything?"

Cara laughed and brushed her sweat-lank blonde hair back from her eyes. "Of course not. The idea is to give the native something bitter that produces obvious results."

"Giving a physic produces results," Slocum had to agree, "but why make it bitter?"

"All medicine's bitter," said Frieda, looking up from her cards. "You ever take medicine what wasn't awful tastin'?"

"Can't say that I have."

"There, you see?" Frieda Ferguson went back to her fortune telling. Slocum wondered what she saw in her own future. More of Billy, more of Mort Thorogoode's medicine show, more heat and sun?"

"A shame about losing Milo," said Cara. "We need a new gimmick to get people interested. A hook to draw them in to the show. We used a Gila monster for a while. Great ballyhoo until Mort got careless with the dumb son of a bitch and let it loose in the crowd. It actually bit a woman and killed her."

"What'd you do?" Slocum asked, intrigued.

"Had to shoot the Gila monster. Gave the woman a big dose of Doctor Wong's Elixir and told her family she'd recover. Then we hightailed it out of there. Haven't been back to Prescott in damn near three years. Think they've forgot about it by now?"

Slocum marvelled at Cara O'Connell. She seemed perfectly suited for this life.

"Think you'll catch up with the men who shot you and get all that money back?" the blonde asked in a voice so low only Slocum heard. His hard green eyes locked with her softer ones.

"Never said anything about money."

"Has to be. Bank robbery here and there. Word travels in this part of the country. Nothing else to do but gossip. The Nathan gang robbed an El Paso del Norte bank, I heard tell back in Hot Springs. Man answering your description helped out."

Slocum looked out the back door of the wagon. His hand flashed to his pistol, then stopped there. The butt of his Colt Navy remained cold in spite of the desert heat, but it didn't come close to matching the coldness he felt in the middle of his belly.

The thought of getting out the back of the wagon, saddling his horse, and riding like hell ran through Slocum's mind. He pushed it away. Both horses' ears were laid back, indicating they were tired. He'd never be able to get far enough away in this punishing heat.

"What's wrong, John?" asked Cara, seeing the way he stiffened.

"Apaches. Caught sight of a dust cloud behind us. Nothing else would kick up a fuss like that."

"Might just be a dust devil," said Frieda, not even looking up from her cards. "This time of year, the dust is at its worst."

Slocum had been through West Texas dust storms and had seen the cyclonic pillars of dust rising two hundred feet and more into the sky—the dust devils—and this was neither. He'd seen too many dust clouds kicked up by horses' hooves not to recognize them. And who but the Apaches would be out in the middle of the day in such numbers?

Another thought came and went. It might be a posse. He decided against this, since the posse would have had to come from Hot Springs. He didn't see anyone in that sleepy little town getting agitated enough to come after them for Larouche's death. A drifter, and one riding with the likes of Henry Nathan, would never be missed or mourned.

Apaches. That had to be Apaches coming up behind the wagon.

Cara spoke up. "I think John might be right, Frieda. Doesn't look like a storm. See how the sides are breaking off, just like they're trying to get us boxed in."

Slocum was astounded at how easily the two women accepted this.

"The Apaches have been raising hell along here for months. When I was in El Paso the townspeople spoke of the soldiers from Fort Bliss tracking down Indians. Both Mescalero and Western Apaches."

"The Western are farther over in Arizona right now and the Jicarilla are north," said Cara. "These must be Mescalero."

"You don't care?" Slocum's heart thumped power-fully in his chest now. He didn't especially want to die, but when he did it'd be with a sixgun in hand and fighting to the last.

"The Mescaleros are easier to get along with. How long do you think before they overtake us?" Cara asked.

"Not more'n an hour at this rate." *Not more'n an hour to live,* Slocum mentally added. He had seen what the Indians did to interlopers. Eyelids cut off, then staked out on the hot sand to stare into the sun. Mouth tied open and filled with honey, then buried neck deep for the ants to devour from the inside out. Skinned alive. The Apaches had imaginations which lent themselves well to torturing white men.

"They don't bother us." Cara patted down her sweaty hair and stood. "Better let Mort know. It'll take him a while to get ready." On the way to the front of the wagon, she poked Billy Ferguson hard in the ribs. "Wake up, you good for nothing. You got to drive for a while."

The man stirred and tried to roll over. This time his wife prodded him. Cara O'Connell rapped smartly on

the sliding panel between the driver's seat and the back
of the wagon. It opened and Thorogoode's mouth appeared. Slocum didn't hear what the man said but he
could read his lips. Thorogoode was not happy at being
disturbed. Cara spoke rapidly. Slocum almost tumbled
from the bunk when Thorogoode unexpectedly halted the
mules.

Grumbling, Thorogoode came into the back of the
wagon. "Go drive," he told Billy, but the man had suc-
ceeded in rolling over and going back to sleep. Slocum
guessed it was more of a coma than a sleep from the
quantity of liquor he'd put away.

"I'll drive," Slocum volunteered. "You want me to
stay on the road?"

"No," sneered Thorogoode, "I want you to get us lost
out in the middle of the goddamn desert." Grumbling
even louder, Thorogoode began rummaging through the
racks for his makeup.

"Straight ahead, then," said Slocum, not wanting to
make an issue of it. Thorogoode's pallor astounded him,
but, like the others, he showed no fear of the rapidly
approaching Apaches.

"I'll keep you company," said Cara.

"The hell you will. I want Princess Lotus Blossom
with me."

Slocum indicated that Cara shouldn't object. Alone,
he dropped from the tailgate of the wagon and went
around, checking the wheels, his two horses, the mules,
and finally the reins. Everything in good condition. Slocum
climbed into the box and "gee-hawed" the mules. They
began pulling sluggishly. Slocum wiped sweat out of his
eyes and wondered at the animals' endurance in this heat.
It was foolhardy to keep travelling during the day, but
Thorogoode had plans he wasn't revealing.

Slocum just hoped those plans didn't include getting
them all scalped.

The Indians caught up with the wagon less than an

hour later. Slocum used all his willpower to keep from reaching to his left hip and pulling out his Colt when two Apaches raced up on either side of his team and grabbed the reins. He halted the wagon and simply sat staring at the braves.

It might have been a hundred and twenty out on the desert. Slocum turned polar cold inside when he saw the white and yellow lines on the braves' cheeks: warpaint. Everything he'd heard in El Paso del Norte was right.

Slocum stared straight ahead, not blinking, not twitching a muscle, when one brave rode back and prodded him in the ribs with a feather-decked war lance. The Apache applied pressure. The sharp tip of the lance penetrated skin and drew blood. Slocum still didn't move. The tip bit deeper and pain started now. The wound where Nathan had gunned him down throbbed like a son of a bitch.

Slocum gulped when the brave let out a loud shriek. He thought he was a goner, but the brave withdrew and went to the rear of the wagon. Slocum looked around cautiously and saw that the other Apaches had gone to the back of the wagon, too. He slid open the tiny window and got a good view all the way to the tiny stage. Both Thorogoode and Cara struck poses in their Doctor Wong and Princess Lotus Blossom costumes. The sunlight turned the yellow dye to a sickly jaundice color, but the Indians appeared mesmerized by the pair.

"Gleetings flom Cerestial Empire," said Doctor Wong, bowing deeply. "I lecognize blave warrior chief." Another bow. Princess Lotus Blossom dropped to her knees and kowtowed, banging her head on the stage three times. While the Apache leading the band tried to keep his face impassive, Slocum saw the brave was pleased at this obeisance.

"You gleat warrior, but there are ploblems."

"We win!" shouted the brave, his lance thrust at the sky, as if it were the enemy.

"Ancient wisdom say you lose." Before the Apache

could build an appropriately angry response, Doctor Wong went on smoothly, "Unress humble fliends aid you with velly, velly powelful magic." Doctor Wong bowed.

The Apaches exchanged glances. One nodded. Slocum got the feeling that this was part of a ritual they always went through. If so, Doctor Wong knew how to placate them. They only pretended anger to get some of Doctor Wong's Elixir.

At least, Slocum hoped that were true.

"You need Doctor Wong's Marvelous Elixir of Life, Catarrh Remedy and Hair Restorer," Thorogoode said in a singsong voice. The man acted out his role as Doctor Wong as good as any actor on the stage. "One sip and you are invincible. Two and . . . no enemy can harm you!"

This produced a real stir among the braves. One rode closer and banged his lance against the side of the wagon. Slocum had his Colt halfway out of his holster before realizing it. He slipped it back in slowly, letting Doctor Wong do his ballyhoo.

"Want much of this magic," declared the leader.

"Not needed, especially for one already as blave as you," insisted Doctor Wong. "One bottle. Slay many enemies. Many, *many* enemies."

Slocum saw Billy Ferguson start to stir. The drunken man rolled the wrong way on the bunk and landed heavily on the wagon floor. It jolted him to semiconsciousness.

"Billy, stay there," Slocum whispered. But the man was still too groggy to understand. He rose and stumbled out into the bright sunlight and full view of the Indians.

Slocum had his gun out this time, ready to shoot if any of the braves made a move for the drunk.

Doctor Wong took a quick swig from the bottle he held in his hand, then shouted at Billy, "Die!"

Startled, Billy Ferguson stepped back, missing the edge of the stage. He fell with arms flailing and landed hard on the sun-baked sand. A dull thud told of his head striking a rock.

"Enemies die when used with Doctor Wong's Elixir,"

said Thorogoode. "And fliends plosper! You fliend?"

The brave nodded solemnly, his dark eyes darting back and forth between the fallen Billy Ferguson and Doctor Wong.

"You plosper. And *your* enemies die!"

One brave pointed down at Billy. The war leader nodded curtly. Slocum waited for the lance to rise and fall, entering Billy's chest.

Again Doctor Wong came to the rescue. He held up his hand to stop the brave. "Do not tamper with magics."

Princess Lotus Blossom rose and made a quick gesture. Fire erupted from her fingertips. This spooked the Indians' horses.

"Doctor Wong have many magics. For fliends. You fliends?" When he got the quick nods, he smiled. "Take Doctor Wong's Elixir. Not too much. Just sip. Kill enemies!"

Doctor Wong began dispensing the bottles, one to each brave, since they shied away from Princess Lotus Blossom. Cara stood quietly at one side of the stage, where she could protect Billy if the need arose. When the war leader came to take the bottle, Slocum heard Doctor Wong say, "For my velly, *velly* good fliend, two bottle."

Slocum couldn't help but wonder if Doctor Wong wasn't going to try to sell the Apache a magical truss and syphilis medicine, too. Doctor Wong did not press his luck. The Indians had received what they sought. With his magic aiding them, they would go forth to find others to scalp.

Slocum didn't like that, but he did cotton to the idea of keeping his own hair and being allowed to continue on his way unharmed.

The Indians and Doctor Wong talked a few minutes longer, then they rode off. Never had Slocum been so happy to see a dust cloud.

Cara came around and climbed up into the box beside

him. "What are you waiting for, John?" she asked. "We've got another forty miles to go before we reach San Augustine. Mort wants to be there by sometime tomorrow." Cara made a grand gesture with her hand and flames gushed forth. She laughed delightedly and explained, "Flash paper. It impresses the Indians."

"Impresses the hell out of me," admitted Slocum.

He snapped the reins and got the mules moving. Even they pulled with greater determination now, as if they realized how narrow the escape had been. Slocum didn't even complain about the heat. After all, he was still alive to suffer through it.

6

San Augustine was even dustier and smaller than Hot
Springs. Slocum didn't see how the medicine show could
make a dollar here, much less the big money Thorogoode
muttered about constantly.

"You worry too much, John," Cara told him. "We
know our business. Even though there're problems with
Mort, he's one of the best."

Slocum studied the owner of the show and wondered
about what problems Cara referred to. There hadn't been
enough water for Thorogoode to wash off the yellow
dye; he had stayed Doctor Wong since their encounter
with the Apaches. Now that they were camped on the
outskirts of San Augustine, there was no need for him
to want to clean off the dye.

But under the yellow Slocum knew there was only an
unhealthy pallor. Never had he seen any man look so
poorly without turning belly-up dead soon after. Thorogoode seemed in good enough condition other than this.
At times he was downright nasty, at others moody and

71

silent, but never did he give the impression that his mysterious affliction would kill him any time soon.

"We're changing the ballyhoo," Thorogoode said suddenly. "I want a bath. I want to get out of this makeup."

"But, Mort," Cara said, going to him, "what will we do? We're Doctor Wong's Travelling Medicine Show."

"I'll think of something. Doctor Wong is wearing thin. Time to try another pitch."

"We should have worked on this before we got into town," she said angrily. "I don't have time to learn new lines. And I'm not sure I remember enough of the mind-reading codes to—"

"I'll think of something." With that, Mort Thorogoode closed the subject. The man stormed off toward the stables and the small stock pond behind. It wouldn't be long before Thorogoode got rid of his Doctor Wong makeup.

"Can't say I understand this," said Slocum. "You're successful with the Chinaman pitch. Why does he want to change now?"

"Good enough time, I suppose," said Cara. "San Augustine is hardly going to make us all rich. If we don't pull it off, we can change the pitch around before we reach New Albuquerque."

"We're going to Socorro before Albuquerque," said Frieda. "I heard Mort say so this afternoon."

"He ought to tell me these things," Cara said, her anger mounting. "I don't much like surprises."

Slocum saw the cracks forming in the medicine show's tight alliances. Billy had recovered from his fall with a knot the size of a goose egg on the back of his head. He seemed to blame them all for it, though it had helped convince the Apaches of the power of the elixir. Frieda eyed Billy with suspicion ever since he had returned so drunk—or was he drunk? Slocum wondered if Billy Ferguson and Mort Thorogoode didn't have other vices. Both men's complexions were sickly.

"Be just our luck that we need a business license,"

complained Cara. "Every jerkwater town tries to push through ordinances like that. Just another way for the sheriff to make an extra dollar or two."

"Want me to find out for you? I want to look around." Slocum didn't miss the avid expression on Cara's face. Her green eyes seemed to come alive again.

Slocum considered getting on his horse and riding on out. Things with Cara O'Connell might get too complicated. She obviously saw him as a ticket to a better life— one without Mort Thorogoode. If he had a hefty stack of greenbacks, all the better. Slocum wanted to tell the pretty blonde that he was a long way from getting the share of the money due him. He had to settle accounts with Henry Nathan.

If Nathan had any of the money left, all the better. Slocum wasn't about to let it blow off into the sunset if he could claim it for his own. He'd worked hard for it, taken risks, gotten himself shot up. And Nathan had shown himself to be more of a snake than even the dead rattler, Milo. Milo's fangs had been pulled. Nathan shot down Slocum and probably gunned down Walt Larouche, too.

"I'll be back soon," Slocum said.

"Wait!" Cara came over, threw her arms around his neck, and kissed him soundly.

"What was that for?" he asked.

"When you return," she said softly, "there'll be more. Lots more."

He couldn't help himself. Slocum smiled and nodded, going off feeling damned good. It hardly mattered if he found Nathan or even picked up the bushwhacker's scent. He had enough in Cara O'Connell to keep him occupied for a few more days.

San Augustine citizens milled about, trying to keep activity to a minimum. Even when the sun went down and the desert winds turned cooler, it was too hot to do much more than sit on the wood-plank sidewalk, spit, and whittle a mite. Slocum found the saloon, but it wasn't going to open for another hour, after most folks had had time for supper. That told him more about San Augustine than asking ever could have. This wasn't a town that catered to drifters or trailmen. The local trade made up the biggest portion of the saloon business, and the saloon-keeper didn't want to cause any trouble by stirring up the town's soberer folk.

Slocum found the sheriff's office. A deputy snored loudly at the side of the adobe jail. He didn't bother waking the man. Inside, Slocum found a dusty office with several rifle racks mounted on the dried mud brick walls. Not a one of the rifles looked as if it had been oiled, much less fired, in the past year. He saw visible spots of rust. In this dry climate that meant total lack of use or care. San Augustine didn't look to be much of a town for illegal goings-on.

"Sheriff, I'm with Doctor Wong's Travelling Medicine Show," he said to the burly man behind the battered desk made out of old wood planking.

"You don't say." The sheriff turned a florid, profusely sweating face toward Slocum. The eyes narrowed as he studied this unwanted annoyance in the middle of his afternoon *siesta*.

"Wanted to find out if there were any permits required for puttin' on a show."

"Permits?" the sheriff asked, as if he'd never thought of such a thing. Then a gleam came to his eyes. Slocum had seen greed before but seldom this poorly disguised. "Course there are permits. Lots of them. Land use permits, excise taxes to be paid, then there's a license fee for just being a performer." The sheriff hesitated as he studied Slocum more carefully. Nothing about John-Slocum spoke of performer, not with the gun slung at his left hip in the cross-draw holster.

"I'm not," Slocum said, answering the unvoiced question. "Just travelling through with them on the way up to Albuquerque. Didn't want to travel the *Jornado del Muerte* alone."

"Gets nasty this time of summer," the sheriff said. "Apaches everywhere. The heathens are shootin' up settlers as far north as Raton, I hear, though they seem to have passed us by."

"We ran into a war party. About thirty, I'd say."

The sheriff's eyes narrowed even more, and his face turned beet red. Slocum wondered if the man might hurt himself trying to think.

"How'd you get close enough to count the bastards?"

Slocum laughed. "They came to us."

"Take off your Stetson." Slocum did so, and the sheriff looked even more puzzled. "You're still wearing your hair and you say they came to you?"

"Even the heathens know the value of Doctor Wong's Elixir," Slocum said with a straight face.

The sheriff broke out laughing now.

"That's a good one. You sucked me right into it, you did. A good one." The sheriff took out a grimy bandana and wiped sweat from his face. "Convinced me to let you put on your show. The license is only . . . one hundred dollars. In gold. None of those Yankee greenbacks. Gold."

"That's mighty steep, isn't it, Sheriff?"

"You look to take a goodly piece of San Augustine's money away with you. This is the town's way of making sure some of it stays where it belongs."

Slocum didn't dispute the claim, though he figured it was the sheriff's way of making sure he supplemented the paltry salary his townfolk paid.

"Don't have that kind of money on me. Have to go check with the owner. He'll get back to you on this."

"See that he does. No license, no show." The sheriff turned back to more important duties. His snores rivalled those of the deputy still asleep outside before Slocum closed the wood door to the jail.

On his way back to the medicine show, Slocum stopped

and leaned against a splintery hitching post. The old men sitting on the sidewalk had set up a table and played dominoes. One canted his head to the side and studied Slocum.

"You play Moon, mister?"

"Have sometimes. Prefer Forty-two."

The old man nodded. "My choice, too, but Luke here don't like Forty-two." Luke didn't stir. He continued to study the lay of the dominoes as if the time of the Second Coming was to be revealed to him through the black tiles and white dots.

"You happen to see any other strangers in town lately?" Slocum asked after a decent interval. The old man dropped a domino onto the table and sat back, a crooked smile on his face.

"Not before you showed up. Not many strangers come through San Augustine. We're out of the way. Got to cross the mountains and git back on the other side 'fore you find many travellin' north or south. Only thing we got going for us on this side is good wells. Over there, up toward Socorro, they get their water from the Rio Grande. Piss-poor water."

"But not in San Augustine?" asked Slocum.

"Not here," the old man said. Luke already shuffled the dominoes for another game.

"Then you haven't seen anyone else through here in a week or so?"

"Closer to a month. The Apaches keep down the travellin', too. Damn redskins." The man sucked on his toothless gums for a minute, then added, "Some ain't too bad, though. If you keep 'em away from the firewater they ain't so bad."

"Come on out to Doctor Wong's wagon tonight," Slocum said. "Always a good time listening to Doctor Wong and looking at the lovely Princess Lotus Blossom." He bit his tongue when he realized that Thorogoode wanted to try new routines here.

"Might break my winnin' streak," the old man said. "Doubt if I'll go. Doubt if many will."

"If you change your mind . . ." Slocum let the sentence trail off. The man had already turned back to his dominoes, chortling at a successful play.

Slocum picked up the pace as he returned to the wagon. If Nathan hadn't come this way, that meant he had to have gone on to Socorro. Doctor Wong's medicine show headed for Socorro after it left this tiny town. Slocum decided to stay with Thorogoode—and Cara—for another few days. If they were all heading in the same direction, why not enjoy their company?

Slocum thought a bit more on this. Cara was a delight, but the tension was mounting between her and Thorogoode and between Thorogoode and Slocum. With Billy and Frieda there was nothing but animosity. Billy Ferguson hardly stayed sober. And he shared with Mort Thorogoode that curious pallor, intensely bright eyes, and oddly nervous behavior. Slocum might be getting himself in for more trouble than he intended if he stayed too long with the show, but the lure remained.

Cara O'Connell was a delight to hold. Her body seemed to be perfectly molded to his when they were together, but she wanted more from him than a brief fling. She saw Slocum as being wealthy when he recovered the bank money and her way out of Thorogoode's clutches. Slocum didn't much like that idea. He was no one's meal ticket, and when he got the money from the robbery, he wasn't about to share it with anyone. The risk had been too great.

He stopped just short of the brightly painted wagon. Billy Ferguson was putting a new banner on the side. Doctor Wong had changed to Doctor Denton's Marvelous Travelling Medicine Show.

Cara saw him and waved. "Like the change?" she asked. Slocum smiled slowly, then nodded.

"That what you wear now?"

Cara pirouetted for him, the indecently short skirt spiralling out from her slender legs. The mere sight of so much female would start riots in most frontier towns. Even here in sleepy San Augustine it might cause a stir.

"Nothing more'n this. The idea is that Mort gets 'em interested, I get them *real* interested, and then he sells them. Billy and Frieda can work the crowd, and we all ought to do just fine."

"Maybe not," Slocum said. He couldn't take his eyes off the woman. He couldn't make up his mind whether he'd ever seen anyone prettier. Probably, but he couldn't remember when or where. "You're too good for a town like this."

"What do you mean?"

"The sheriff wants a hundred dollars for a license to perform."

"We're not actors!" Cara stormed. "We are dispensing beneficial potions for the ailing populace of this fine town." She stopped and smiled almost shyly. "I like that. Think I'll tell Mort. Maybe he can use it in his pitch."

"The sheriff might be a real problem. He looks the kind who can be bought, and if he isn't he likes to cause trouble."

"A hundred is out of the question. I'm sure Mort will agree. Five is too much, but we'd go that far to buy off a hick-town sheriff. Ten in a city like Santa Fe."

Slocum started to ask what they intended to do when Mort Thorogoode came onto the stage. He'd dressed in his gray morning suit and silk top hat. He looked for all the world like a riverboat gambler rather than a patent-medicine salesman. Mort nodded to Frieda, who began banging on a small drum.

"Step right up, ladies and gentlemen. You might not know it, but your lives are nearing an end. Yes, that's what I said, you don't have much longer to live."

Slocum pulled Cara aside and said impatiently, "Better stop him. The sheriff..."

"You worry too much, John. No sheriff's going to stop the sale of Doctor Denton's Curing Potion and Intestinal Eliminant. Not after Billy spent almost twenty minutes doing up the labels."

Slocum watched glumly as they worked the crowd. At first, only a handful of people came to listen to Thorogoode tell them how soon they would die without his potions. The crowd grew until fifty people pressed close to the stage, most of them clutching their dollar bills to purchase a large-sized bottle of the good doctor's elixir. It took less than an hour to make the pitch and remove the surplus money from circulation in San Augustine's economy.

Thorogoode sat on the tailgate kicking his feet back and forth like a small child. He had undergone another of his mood shifts, and now he laughed and joked with Cara and the others. Even to Slocum he was cordial rather than remote.

"Seventy-four dollars. Not bad, not bad at all for a jerkwater place like this. Cara, let's me and you go find the best restaurant in town."

Slocum started to tell Thorogoode about the sheriff's insistence on the hundred-dollar license, but the man waved him off. "Later, Slocum. We'll deal with him later. Just you be sure the mules are hitched up and ready to go and the water barrels have enough in them to get us to Socorro. You do that? Good man." He slapped Slocum on the shoulder. Cara gave his arm a gentle squeeze as she brushed by, then took Thorogoode's extended arm and walked off with him in search of a good restaurant.

Billy and Frieda were inside the wagon doing whatever they did after one of the demanding medicine shows. Slocum saw the wisdom in being ready to leave San Augustine at a moment's notice. He got the mules ready, then filled the empty water barrels from the stock tank. When he finished, he decided to go get himself a bite to eat. While neither Thorogoode nor Cara had given him any more money, he had twenty cents left. It would be enough for a plate of beans and a slice of bread.

As he approached the town's only restaurant, he saw trouble ahead. Slocum picked up the pace but still arrived a few seconds after the sheriff and his deputy entered. The two stood for a moment, heads revolving around like blades on a windmill. When they sighted Mort Thorogoode, Slocum thought all hell would break loose. From the empty plates strewn around on the table, Thorogoode had obviously finished a very expensive meal.

Slocum could almost read the sheriff's mind: *That shoulda been my meal.*

He slipped the thong off the Colt's smooth hammer and started to pull out his gun when Thorogoode began hacking and coughing. Cara rose and slapped him on the back, but it did no good. Water didn't help. Nothing seemed to.

"What's wrong with him?" demanded the sheriff.

"Tuberculosis," Cara said. "He's a mighty sick man. The last doctor who looked at him said he hasn't more than a few months to live. With all the hardships out here, maybe not even that."

Slocum frowned. Thorogoode looked as strong as a horse, in spite of his pallor.

"T-tuberculosis?" muttered the deputy, taking a quick step back. "That's catching. We seen too many die from it, Sheriff."

"Shut up." The sheriff turned to Thorogoode, who had controlled his coughing seizure. The wide eyes and gray-white skin were those of a man dying. "I don't care if you die next Thursday, you're gonna pay the license fee for puttin' on your show right now. One hundred dollars. Gold. Or you spend the next month in my jailhouse."

"Sheriff, no!" protested Cara, wringing her hands and looking pitiful. "It would kill him! He couldn't stand it!"

Thorogoode began coughing again. Others in the room

edged away. One knocked over his chair in his haste to leave the room. Tuberculosis killed off too many. They didn't want to be around anyone with it. They might catch it and die themselves.

"Sheriff," the deputy said, tugging at the other man's sleeve. "I don't want to catch no disease." Thorogoode turned and coughed directly at the deputy. The frightened man almost bolted and ran from the room.

"Please, sir," said Cara. "Let us finish our meal. It is his only pleasure. His *only* pleasure. You see, the disease has effected many parts of his body." She solemnly nodded when the deputy started to name the other afflicted areas.

"Jehoshaphat!" The deputy backed away now, his face pale.

"Finish," the sheriff said with ill grace, "but don't be long." He glanced over at the frightened owner of the restaurant, who smiled weakly. This had destroyed his trade for the night, such as it was in San Augustine.

Slocum slipped in and stood to one side as the sheriff and deputy left. He figured Cara and Thorogoode would hurry out the back way. He would join them and they could be out of town before the sheriff knew what was happening. To Slocum's surprise, Mort Thorogoode sat back in his chair, loosened his belt another notch, and asked what was available for dessert.

It surprised Slocum even more when Thorogoode ordered the watermelon. Out here, even having it on the menu was amazing. The price quoted for it was even more so, but Thorogoode only smiled and nodded. When the thick slab of red-meated fruit was set in front of him, he began eating with gusto.

Cara excused herself and came over to where Slocum watched. "Everything ready, John?"

"What's he doing? He doesn't act like that sheriff's going to be madder'n a wet hen. If we all don't get tarred and feathered, it'll be a first-class miracle."

"Mort knows what he's doing. Poor baby. That tuberculosis and all."

"Never heard him so much as sneeze, much less cough."

The cold glare Cara gave him told Slocum to keep his peace. She smiled then and joined Thorogoode as the man was leaving. Slocum followed a few paces behind, ready to use his Colt. He didn't see any way around it. The sheriff wanted his hundred dollars and Thorogoode obviously had spent quite a bit of the seventy-four he'd collected on the meal.

"You, Doc," said the sheriff, taking Thorogoode by the arm. "We're going to my office for a little talk."

"Careful, sir, his disease. The tuberculosis is deadly." Cara solicitously held Thorogoode's other arm.

The sheriff tried not to act as if this mattered, but he released Thorogoode and stepped back half a pace. The deputy almost ran on ahead.

"He's bad off, Sheriff. It was so good of you to let him finish the meal," Cara O'Connell said. "I . . . I just don't think he's going to make it. He . . . he's dying. Now. Of the dread disease."

"Don't lie to me," the sheriff snapped. But he quieted down when Thorogoode began coughing. This time the seizure made the one in the restaurant seem puny in comparison. The man's entire body quaked with every cough.

"My guts. Oh, my insides! I feel everything coming loose. I'm dying. Sweet Jesus, comfort me, I'm dying!"

The sheriff tried to hold Thorogoode up when the man started sinking slowly to the street. The lawman jerked back when Thorogoode spat up a liquid red gob."

"His lungs!" shrieked Cara. "It's happening! His lungs are coming out!"

The sheriff released Thorogoode and jerked back, mouth open and eyes wide. Thorogoode coughed and hacked and spat out another mouthful of slimy red matter.

"Goddamn, you get this man out of my town right now. Right now, you hear? I don't want no one dying of tuberculosis in San Augustine. We ain't got a doctor."

"Epidemic," murmured Cara.

"Get that sorry son of a bitch out of town *now!*" cried the sheriff.

Slocum took this to be his cue. He rushed over and helped Thorogoode to his feet. On shaky legs, the medicine-show owner walked along. When they got back to the wagon, Thorogoode wiped the red slime off his chin.

"Waste of good watermelon," he complained, "but worth it." He threw back his head and laughed. "Get in the box, Slocum, and get us out of here. On to Socorro. Doctor Denton's Marvelous Travelling Medicine Show must move on!"

Slocum shook his head. And he'd thought robbing a bank was a crime. These people could teach a fox to steal chickens. Slocum climbed up and whacked the reins onto the mules' rumps. All the way out of town the wagon rocked from Thorogoode's loud, fake coughs. Then came only laughter.

7

Doctor Wong's—now Doctor Denton's—Marvelous Travelling Medicine Show zigzagged back and forth across the barren desert until Slocum thought they would all die under the blazing sun. Thorogoode seemed to have lost his sense of direction and didn't even notice. He sat up in the box, his chin tipping forward until it touched his chest. How any man could sleep in this heat and with the bouncing of the wagon was beyond Slocum. But Mort Thorogoode had no trouble.

Three days out of San Augustine, they crossed the mountains and caught sight of the Rio Grande again. The shallow, muddy river wound back and forth in its narrow band of green. From their vantage point in the foothills, Slocum estimated that it was as long as a two-day trip to reach the river, if they found a good road in that direction. More than likely, it would be three days of trailblazing on their part.

He didn't want to consider how it would be if Thorogoode lost sight of the river and started meandering all over the desert, like he had been the better part of the last three days.

"What's wrong with him?" asked Slocum.

Cara glanced around nervously. The question obviously upset her.

"Nothing," she said too forcefully, as if trying to convince herself. "Mort's been under a lot of strain. We all have. You saw what happened back in San Augustine. The sheriff might have got it into his head to put us all in jail."

"Unless I miss my guess, Thorogoode's got money enough to have paid him off. Thorogoode just didn't want to spend it."

"We've been doing all right," Cara admitted.

"And Thorogoode enjoyed that run-in. I saw his face after we left. He *enjoyed* it. What's the strain? Being in the desert and running short of water? We ought to have been in Socorro by now."

"Mort doesn't know this part of the *Jornado del Muerte* very well." Slocum saw that this sounded lame even to the woman's own ears. She rushed on, saying, "Been a long time since we passed this way. You can't blame Mort."

"No blame. I reckon I'll be parting company with you in Socorro and going on my own way."

Cara came over to Slocum and sat by his side. In the heat, there was no way she could be seductive. This didn't stop her from trying. Her sweaty fingers stroked over his cheek, down his throat, and to the opened front of his shirt. Her fingers worked tiny spirals in the perspiration-matted hair on his chest.

"You think you know where your partners are?" she whispered.

"I think they're ahead of us and putting more distance between us every day." He swallowed hard, fighting down the anger at Nathan. "And they're not my partners."

"Could I be your partner? In everything?"

"Why are you so eager to leave Thorogoode?" he asked bluntly. "The man doesn't treat you bad. You even said you have diamonds and fancy gowns and go to all the high-society places when you get into the big cities. I can't offer you anything like that. Even if I got all the money due me—plus Nathan's portion—I can't match what Thorogoode looks to make on this trip to Santa Fe."

Slocum thought of all the eager hands thrusting the crumpled dollar bills at the patent medicine peddler. The vile brew he sold them would give them bellyaches, but when the next show came through they'd all come back for more of the "medicine." He shook his head. Robbing banks with a gun seemed more honest work to him than this. Leastways, he didn't play on people's gullibility.

"Mort is different from other men," Cara said slowly, choosing her words with care. "And you're different, too, but in a nicer way." Her hand moved up his chest and stroked through his raven-dark hair. Slocum didn't like the way he responded to her overtures. Her game was apparent. Get him involved and he'd do anything she wanted, which included taking her away from Mort Thorogoode.

"We're going to kill the mules unless Thorogoode stops to rest," Slocum said, pulling away. Sweat ran in steady, tickling rivers down his body. The stifling desert heat was almost more than he could bear inside the wagon. The animals outside had to be damned near dead by now. Billy and Frieda slept on their bunks as if the sun beating down meant nothing. Maybe to them this was usual. Slocum would have preferred travelling the desert at night when it was cooler.

Without a steady supply of water, they would all perish in short order.

"Mort gets like this," the woman told him. Cara leaned back on the narrow bunk and eyed Slocum with unabashed desire. "There's no telling him different, either."

"I'm going to try."

Cara tried to hold Slocum back, but he'd made up his mind. Being cruel to people was one thing; punishing the animals needlessly was another. They couldn't fight back and, from a more selfish point of view, those mules had to get all of them out of the desert. Kill the mules and everybody died.

Slocum agilely swung around the side of the wagon, gripping at the bolts where the new banner hung. He heaved and got himself onto the roof of the wagon. The heat dancing off the top caused a shimmering that made everything look insubstantial. Slocum almost burned his hands on the roof as he made his way to the front. Even with the driver's box, he swung over the edge and down onto the seat.

Thorogoode didn't look the least bit surprised at this sudden entrance. He just stared ahead, eyes fixed on the horizon. Slocum thought the man might have died up here and his body gone stiff already. Then Thorogoode brushed a fly crawling along the top of his ear. This was about the only indication that he was still alive.

"Let's give the mules a rest," Slocum said. He pitched his voice in such a way that the sting of command went along with the words.

Thorogoode turned listless eyes toward Slocum. He'd heard, but gave little indication of being able to act. His pallor had increased to the point of looking like a corpse. Slocum thought he sweated a great deal; Thorogoode was completely soaked in his own juices.

"Hot, isn't it?" Thorogoode asked. His voice came in a flat monotone.

"You feeling all right?" Slocum asked. "Want me to take over the driving chores for a while?"

Without a word, Thorogoode handed over the reins. Slocum turned and surveyed the terrain. A small stand of cypress hinted at a cool resting spot. He turned the mules toward it. They almost broke into a gallop getting there.

"We'll rest till sundown," Slocum told the owner of the show. "Give the animals a chance to recuperate."

No argument, no words from Thorogoode. He just sat and stared as if his soul had fled. Or his sanity.

Slocum swung down and unharnessed the mules. While the small stand of cypress included a couple of cottonwoods, he didn't find any small spring bubbling up to the surface. The trees' roots might go down fifty or a hundred feet for water. Some mesquite, he'd heard tell, dropped their taproot as much as five hundred feet. The only way of controlling mesquite was to do as the Comanche did—burn it level with the ground every year. No amount of work would ever destroy the roots.

Slocum brushed down the mules and his two horses. None appeared grateful to him. The heat was almost more than they could bear. Finished tending the animals, Slocum went around to the back of the wagon. Thorogoode had already climbed into one of the bunks and slept fitfully. He twitched and jerked and his mouth made funny movements that weren't smiles or grimaces. If Slocum hadn't known better, he would have thought Thorogoode was possessed of a demon.

Cara climbed down and looked around. She found a nice spot and pointed. Slocum silently followed and settled down beside her. The slight breeze blowing helped cool them down. The sweat evaporated almost instantly now. But it was still damned hot.

"What's wrong with Thorogoode?" he asked bluntly. "Something's not right with him."

"Don't worry about Mort," Cara said. "He always manages to come out just fine. I'm more worried about Billy. He woke up." She made this sound like the end of the world.

"So?"

"So he's in a mean mood."

Slocum sighed and lounged back, hat over his eyes. The ground was cool under him and he wanted nothing more than to take a nap himself. The heat had sapped his strength. If only he'd confronted Thorogoode earlier, they might have been able to rest. As it was, they had only a few hours until evening. He wouldn't have any reason not to travel on then.

A woman's cry was cut off by a meaty *thud!*

Slocum sat up, hat flying, hand on pistol. He looked around the tiny grove and saw Billy Ferguson drawing his hand back to hit his wife again. They'd left the wagon and had gone fifty yards in the direction away from Cara and Slocum.

"John, don't," cautioned Cara. "Billy's got the mood on him."

"Hell if I'll let him beat up a woman." Slocum shot to his feet and covered the distance before Billy had time to hit Frieda more than three times. The woman had fallen to her knees and stuggled weakly against Billy's out-of-control anger.

"You slut. You been fucking him again, ain't you? Ain't you?"

He cocked his arm back, but the blow never landed. Slocum caught the fist and held it.

"Try to work this out peaceful-like," Slocum said. He spun Billy Ferguson around. "It isn't polite to beat up on a woman."

"She deserved it." Billy's eyes were bigger than saucers, but the pupils had contracted to tiny pinpoints. The sunlight was bright, but Slocum thought the look on the man's face unnatural. He certainly wasn't able to control his wrath.

"I wasn't sleeping with Mort, honest, Billy. You know I don't do that no more. Please don't hit me again!"

"He won't," Slocum cut in. "Whatever differences you two have are going to be talked out, aren't they?"

Slocum was strong. He didn't expect the surge as Billy jerked free to be so much more powerful than he was. Billy ripped his hand from Slocum's, then landed a crushing blow to the side of the head. Slocum stumbled back and fell to the ground. His head rang like a bell, and a buzzing in his ears told him a mule had upped and kicked him.

Before Slocum could regain his senses, Billy Ferguson swarmed over him like a hill of ants. Fists pounded with no apparent guidance, teeth bit, and feet kicked. Slocum managed to roll and get Billy under him. The expression on the man's face was one of total rage.

With a convulsive surge, Billy threw Slocum off him. Both men came to their feet, circling, looking for advantage.

"Don't kill him, Slocum, please don't!" pleaded Frieda. "He's a good man, except when he's like this."

Billy wasn't armed, but Slocum still considered drawing the Colt and putting a few bullets into the man's body. Billy's arms rippled with muscle. The tendons stood out in bold relief, highlighted by the sunlight filtering through the gray-green leaves of the cottonwoods. He looked like the picture of a Roman gladiator Slocum had seen once. Nothing would stop him short of death.

Billy rushed him and grasped him around the body, pinning Slocum's arms to his sides. Even if Slocum had wanted to pull his gun now, it was too late.

"Kill you, you son of a bitch. Fucking my wife. Teach you. Teach you good!"

The pressure increased and bent Slocum backward. He felt his spine cracking and popping in protest. Every breath he took made the next more difficult. The pressure prevented him from properly inhaling. He was being broken into two and suffocated at the same time. The world spun, then began turning black around the edges. Slocum's vision collapsed to a tiny tunnel.

Finding strength he didn't know he had, Slocum twisted to the side and jerked as hard as he could. His left arm came free, and he got a deep lungful of air. Then came the crushing power of Billy Ferguson's embrace.

"You're gonna die!" shrieked Billy in insane rage.

Slocum didn't try to play fair. He drove his fingers straight into Billy's eyes. The man yelped and dropped him. Slocum fell to one knee, then wound up a punch and delivered it with all his might to Billy's midriff. The blow might have been stronger if he hadn't had so much taken out of him by the bearhug. It was enough to stagger Ferguson back.

Slocum didn't want to trade punches. He'd lose. He kicked out and caught Billy behind the ankle. The man fell heavily. Slocum jumped into the air and landed with both knees in the center of Billy's stomach. The sudden *whoosh!* of air from the fallen man's lungs told the story. Billy rolled onto his side and puked.

Panting, Slocum stood over him, considering a final kick to the head to end it all.

"Billy, Billy, are you all right?" Frieda held the man's head in her lap, stroking the tangled hair. She looked up at Slocum and said, "You didn't have no call to do this. He wouldn't have hurt you none."

"He sure as hell was beating up on you," Slocum snapped. Then he fell silent. If this was all the gratitude he got from the woman, he'd let Billy Ferguson beat the living hell out of her next time. And he didn't doubt for an instant that there'd be a next time, just as there had been a history of this before.

Slocum rejoined Cara, who sat silently.

"Should have known better," Slocum finally said. "Maybe she likes getting beat up. I've heard tell of women like that."

"No," Cara said softly, "she doesn't like it. But Frieda knows it's only Billy's problem doing it. They love each other. It's just that he can't control himself sometimes."

"Problem? What problem?"

Cara swallowed hard and stared over at the Fergusons. "Let's go somewhere else. I'll tell you there."

Slocum found a cool spot at the far edge of the cottonwood stand. Not fifteen feet away, the harsh desert sand started again. Heat bounced and radiated upward off its tawny expanse, but they stayed cool as long as they were under the branches of a cypress.

"So?" demanded Slocum. "What's this problem you're always talking about?"

"Men get bad habits," Cara said slowly. "Billy drinks something fierce, but that's no problem. We always carry enough liquor with us for use in Doctor Wong's elixirs to keep him from getting too rambunctious. If anything, we can use the bottles after he's emptied them."

Slocum stared at the woman, saying nothing. Uncomfortably, Cara O'Connell went on. "Billy's got another vice. He doesn't look at other women. He's content enough with Frieda. He doesn't gamble. Never seen him do more than bet for matchsticks. But he can't stay away from opium."

"Opium? Where'd he get that?"

"We used a goodly portion in some of our patent medicines a while back. He took to smoking it."

"I've seen men who smoked opium. They get all sleepy and drool on themselves. They weren't at all like Billy was back there."

"That's when they smoke the drug. As long as they have a ready supply, everything's fine." A flush came to Cara's pale cheeks. "Only when they don't have it do they get . . . like Billy."

"He's going to kill Frieda one of these days."

Cara only nodded.

"Where do you get it?" Slocum asked. "Get him some more."

"In this part of the country it's harder to come by. We thought we'd got some down in El Paso del Norte, but it turned out to be worthless tar. The man cheated us. There won't be another place to get some until we reach Albuquerque."

"Can he last that long?"

"Billy's able to drink and keep down his urges, but

frankly, John, I don't know if he can make it or not. He's heavily addicted. Sporadic users don't feel the symptoms like he does. He'll smoke three or four pipes just to get ready."

That meant nothing to Slocum. He liked his vices active—drinking, gambling, women.

"If it's any consolation," Cara went on, "he won't even remember you beat him up."

"Or that he was beating up on his wife?"

Cara shook her head. "It's a hard life, travelling with a show. Never having a place to call home. Dodging the law. Seeing how stupid and silly the natives can be. The drugs. These are the things I want to leave behind." Her fingers sought and found Slocum's. She squeezed.

He turned toward her and saw the longing in her eyes. He bent over and lightly kissed her lips. He tasted salty sweat and the grit of dust. Then her lips parted and her tongue stroked along the side of his. All thoughts of sweat and dust were forgotten then.

The woman's arms circled his neck and pulled him down. This embrace was infinitely better than the one that had almost broken his back. Slocum found himself responding now. His breath came harder and his loins burned with need. Slocum grunted when Cara reached down and began unfastening his fly. He rolled onto his back to give her a better chance at getting him free of his cloth prison.

His erection popped out, throbbing and ready.

"So big," she muttered. Cara snaked down his body and took the tip of his manhood into her mouth. She sucked and kissed and licked and did things that gave Slocum more pleasure than he could bear.

He ran his hands through her sweat-lank blonde hair and guided her up and down in the motion he found so exciting. "Can't stand that much longer," he told her. "That mouth of yours knows all the right things to get me hot."

"I don't want to waste a single inch of this," Cara

declared. She pulled her face away from his crotch and hiked up her skirts. With a quick motion, she straddled his waist.

While Slocum couldn't see what was going on for all the layers of cloth, he felt everything. The woman lifted her hips up and reached to guide his pulsing manhood directly to the spot where both of them wanted it the most. Cara sank down slowly, taking his entire length into her steamy interior. She shuddered and closed her eyes.

"You fill me up so much. So big, John darling, so big! I can't stand it!"

Cara put her hands on his chest and levered herself up. He felt his cock slipping slickly from the heated chute. When the woman paused, the purpled arrowhead tip just inside, she gave a twist from side to side that sent Slocum's pulse pounding. Then she slammed back down, grinding their crotches together.

Slowly at first, then with greater insistence, the woman moved. Slocum simply lay back and let her do as she pleased. It suited him just fine, feeling her moving above him, the sensations beating into his body in hot waves of passion. As hot as it was around them and as aching as Slocum's body was from the fight with Billy, he wasn't in much condition to do more than lie back.

Cara moaned and sobbed and moved faster now. She still turned from side to side, but her movements got shakier as pleasure took its toll. Out of control, she rose and dropped with all the strength in her body.

"Oh, yesss!" she moaned, arching her spine and throwing her head back so that her blonde hair dropped onto Slocum's legs. This motion put her over the edge of ecstasy. She quivered and her shoulders and neck flushed with excitement.

Then she started a rhythmic motion up and down that drove Slocum out of his mind. Seconds later, he reached climax, too.

"So good," Cara cooed, leaning forward, letting him

grow limp inside her. She kissed him and put her cheek to his still-heaving chest. "Your heartbeat's so strong. Not like Mort's."

"Is that what's wrong with him? Bad heart?"

Slocum realized he'd said the wrong thing. Cara rose and settled her skirts, rushing off with tears in her eyes. He sighed and lay back, the flies buzzing around over his head. There was so much he didn't understand about the people in this medicine show. He wondered if he'd ever find out the truth.

Even with Cara O'Connell's charms, he wondered if he wanted to find out all their secrets.

8

Slocum avoided Billy Ferguson, and Ferguson avoided Slocum. For both men, this seemed the safest course of action. Slocum studied the man more carefully, though, after all Cara had told him. The shaking hands, the parchment-like skin, the hollow eyes and trapped, haunted expression told of a devil chewing away at Ferguson's guts. Slocum wondered if putting a bullet between Billy's pale eyes and putting him out of his misery might not be the most humane thing to do. After all, it was the least he would do for a horse that broke its leg or any other animal in pain it couldn't bear.

The only good thing about the fight was Mort Thorogoode changing his mind about the breakneck pace they'd been setting. He saw the tension and decided to wait an extra day or two before riding into Socorro. The last thing in the world "Doctor Denton" wanted was trouble among the people in his show who had to work together.

"It's not so bad," Cara told Slocum. "You can learn a few tricks and everything will be just fine."

Slocum was hesitant about being drawn into such scams and hoodwinks. Robbing a man face to face seemed a more honest deed to him than bumping into him and lifting his pocketwatch. There was no way he would ever get good enough to "take out and put back either soft or hard," as Cara called it—lifting a man's wallet and either replacing it with a wad of paper or robbing the wallet and then putting *that* back. Almost instinctively, Slocum checked his own watch. It had belonged to his brother Robert. Shortly after his brother had been killed in the War, Slocum had sent the watch home to his parents. Arriving back in Calhoun County and finding them dead had left a hollowness in him. The watch reminded him of happier times with Robert.

Slocum sighed. He would tar and feather anyone who tried to steal this watch. It wasn't all that expensive, but who could put a value on memories? He remembered how Robert had been so good with horses. There wasn't a cantankerous four-legged son of a buck that Robert couldn't tame. And farm! The man made hay grow just by walking through the fields. If Slocum lived to be a hundred, he'd never have the gift for growing like his brother.

But it had been a mutual admiration. If Robert was the farmer, John Slocum was the natural hunter. Always a good shot, he kept the family supplied with meat, even during the lean years. The old flintlock had seldom failed to bring down a deer or an elk, and his trapping skills were widely praised.

Slocum blinked at the hot desert sun. He'd come a long way from Georgia and his brother's grave at Little Round Top. Pickett had been a damn fool and had taken good men with him.

"You can do anything you want," Cara said to him. Slocum shook himself out of the reverie and focused on her lovely features again. "We don't really need another pitchman. Billy's good enough to work a small crowd by himself."

"So what do you want me to do? I'd be just as happy standing and watching."

"We all work," she said primly, as if he had offended her sense of duty. "You can take care of the drunks. You've worked as a cowboy, haven't you?"

"What? Yes, down in Texas. Over in—"

"It's just the same," Cara interrupted. "You spot the one you want to cut out, then go after him." Before Slocum could ask how, Cara said, "Pretend a horse is standing on your foot. It's happened, hasn't it?"

"Enough," he allowed.

"What do you do?"

"Sort of lean into the horse to get him to lift the hoof."

"Do the same with a drunk. Just lean into him and he moves away. It's perfectly natural and doesn't cause any fuss. Mort doesn't like hecklers when he begins a new pitch."

"Why change? The old one looked like it sold well."

Cara laughed. "We get tired of the same old routine. Imagine me reciting all that about Doctor Wong's virility medicine over and over." She shook her head; the sunlight caught strands of her blonde hair and turned it the color of butterscotch. "You haven't heard me give that one, have you?"

"Can't say that I have. Thorogoode's been the one giving the pitch as Doctor Wong."

"This was an inspired pitch," Cara said, warming to the subject. "In ancient China the men lost their virility. The women began complaining to the Emperor, who saw the problem and offered a ten-thousand-dollar reward for a cure. But there seemed to be no solution to the problem."

She cleared her throat and said, "I go on, building it up a while, until the audience is sure there must not be a Chinaman left in the world. Then I tell them there are millions of them."

"And how did this happen to be if none of the men were able to do their manly duties?" Slocum asked, playing along. He found himself intrigued with the tale in spite of himself. Every bit of it was concocted by Cara's imagination, but she made it seem so real.

"I'm glad you asked, sir," she said, spinning around and pointing her finger at him. "A young man, much like yourself, I'm sure, with inquisitive mind and probing intellect, saw a rare *chu ming* deer. Not for a dozen years had anyone seen it, but there was one—no, two, three! A dozen! A score! Hundreds! All were females following a single male. But how could this be, the young man thought, that a solitary male can keep so many females occupied?"

"How?" Slocum smiled when Cara came closer, running her hand down the front of his shirt, lower, across his crotch, and squeezing until he began to respond. Then she danced away and continued her story.

"That one male was unique! He possessed a secret for virility hitherto unknown. That enterprising young man caught the male and distilled the essence of his gregariousness and won the Emperor's fabulous reward." Cara lowered her voice to a conspiratorial whisper and finished, "This is the secret ingredient of Doctor Wong's Virility Elixir, the same secret given by that young man to his Emperor so many years ago."

"Must have worked. There sure as hell are a lot of Chinamen today," said Slocum.

Cara nodded. "It was a good pitch. When I got rolling with it, I could keep the natives on the hook for an hour or more. Not like Old Ned Hamlin, but still good. He'd harangue his audience for six and eight hours."

"How'd they stand it?"

"He figured they'd believe they really did have kidney problems if they'd stayed that long listening to his guff. He sold a lot of kidney remedy and even Hamlin's Wizard Oil. Ned would rub some of the Wizard Oil on his hands, then do a magic trick. Sell the oil by the gallon after that when he told them they could do the same."

"What was he actually selling?"

"Nothing but liniment. Ned was a great performer, though. Best magician what ever ran a medicine show."

As Cara had talked, she worked on odd concoctions, most of it a mystery to Slocum. He had to ask her what she was doing when she soaked a large sponge in shaving cream. Slocum figured the sponge had to reach a limit of how much it would absorb, but Cara kept at it, then put the sponge out in the hot sun.

"This?" she said. "Part of the Miracle Scrubbing Soap pitch." She banged on the side of the wagon and yelled, "Hey, Mort, you want to come practice the pitch? The sponge is ready."

Slocum sat back under a cottonwood and provided an audience for Thorogoode. The man made his dramatic appearance, even dressed in his Doctor Denton outfit to practice. Thorogoode struck a pose, left hand gripping his lapel, one foot in front of the other, weight rocked onto the back foot.

"Ladies and gentlemen, you are about to witness a miracle. Yes, nothing less than a true miracle. I know," he said, holding up his hand to forestall debate, "it is said that we have departed from the Age of Miracles. I present this fabulous product to you so that you can draw your own conclusions."

Slocum found himself fascinated with the energy in Thorogoode's pitch. The man had touched up his sallow cheeks with tiny smears of rouge. In the bright light he still looked like a walking corpse, but in the evening, when he'd most likely be doing his routine, he would appear the picture of health.

"This is no ordinary bar of soap. This is my very own Doctor Denton's Miracle Soap. Why do I call it a miracle, you ask." Thorogoode gestured. Cara placed a small bucket of water on the edge of the stage. "You will note that I put only a small amount of soap into the bucket."

Thorogoode shaved off a slice from the bar he held

in his hand and dropped it into the bucket. Slocum winced.
Water was precious, even though they'd managed to find
a small spring that fed into the Rio Grande. Their water
barrels were still only a quarter full.

"This, my good friends, is enough to wash down the
walls of a *large* house, do the porch, and still have
enough cleaning suds left to do several small children
and the dog!"

He held out his hand. Cara placed the prepared sponge
in it. Thorogoode dunked the sponge and withdrew it.
Foam frothed up and over the edge of the bucket. He
kept at it for a few seconds until the soapsuds began
piling up at his feet.

"A miracle? Perhaps, ladies and gentlemen. But this
bar of Doctor Denton's Miracle Soap can be yours for
only twenty-five cents. Yes, I know this is expensive,
but it will outlast a dozen—a hundred!—bars of ordinary
soap." The way Thorogoode sneered when he mentioned
"ordinary soap" would definitely tell his assembled audience that they would be doing themselves and their
families a disservice by not rushing up and purchasing
a few bars of the foil-wrapped soap.

Thorogoode wiped his forehead and sat down, carefully avoiding the soapy water oozing over the stage.
"How many bars of soap have you got wrapped up?"

"About a hundred," Frieda told him. "Ran out of the
tin foil."

"That's going to be enough," he decided. "How did
the pitch go?"

"Fine," said Cara, "but you ought to put in something
about how the soap makes ladies' hair lustrous. Appeal
to their vanity as well as their need to keep their urchins
clean."

"Good idea." Thorogoode obviously went over the
pitch again in his mind, adding and changing at the spots
needing it. To Slocum's surprise, Thorogoode asked him,
"You think of anything I ought to add?"

"Might say something about how good it smells. Ladies always appreciate that."

Thorogoode laughed. "We'll make a pitchman out of you yet. There's a reason I didn't mention how wondrous Doctor Denton's Miracle Soap smells. That's because, with every bar of soap you buy, you receive absolutely free a Mexican perfume bean."

"Never heard of it," Slocum said.

Thorogoode snapped his fingers. Frieda handed him a small wooden box. With great care, Thorogoode opened the lid and held a small brown bean between thumb and forefinger.

"Come over here. Tell me what this smells like."

Slocum inhaled, expecting some sort of trick. But he was pleasantly surprised. The fragrance was a relief from trail sweat and the stench of living in his own clothes without a bath for too long.

"Yes, it affects many that way," Thorogoode said solemnly. "This is not just any bean, my friend, but a Mexican perfume bean. Moths seeking out its fragrance have flown for miles, only to die of exhaustion once they have found it in hidden fields in central Mexico."

"Let me guess. This is a pinto bean soaked in perfume," said Slocum.

Thorogoode tossed the bean back into the box and snapped the lid shut. "What else? But the yokels fall all over themselves at the thought of getting something for free."

"What's the soap cost?"

"With the tin foil? Two cents a bar."

"Even so, doesn't look to be much money in this. Even selling a hundred bars only gets you twenty-five dollars."

Thorogoode frowned. "You're right. Have to pitch something else to go along with it."

"You haven't done the limewater pitch in a while," suggested Cara.

"If we can get the limewater, we'll do it. Billy!" the man shouted. "Get your ass moving. I want all the labels off the bottles of Doctor Wong's Magical Elixir changed to Doctor Denton's Catarrh Remedy." Thorogoode swung back up to his feet and disappeared into the wagon.

"What's the limewater routine?" Slocum asked.

"Mort has some native blow through a straw. The limewater turns all milky—sure sign of catarrh, or so we tell him. Then Mort drops in some vinegar and the limewater clears up. A cure!"

"Holding up banks is easier work," Slocum declared. "You folks work too hard at bilking honest folks out of their money."

"The money is interesting," Cara said, "but this is show business. Unless you've done it, there's no way I can tell you how it feels on stage, having the natives eating out of the palm of your hand."

Slocum detected the undercurrent of contempt Cara O'Connell had for the people who were duped into buying the fake products. Yet he sensed some of her excitement at the performance. He had been caught up in Thorogoode's pitch. Even though he'd seen what Cara did with the sponge, he had believed for an instant that the soap was a miracle.

"You are both good at this," he said.

"Good," Cara snorted, shaking her head. "We're terrible. Compared to the best in the business, we're amateurs. Some use Indians for flash—for making what they say seem real. The best of the pitchmen has to be Zach Wyatt. Silvertongue, they called him. His Argentine Murder Mystery pitch was the best." Cara settled down and got a faraway look in her eye. "Silvertongue was the best at muscle reading I ever saw."

"What's that? He figured what a person thought from the way his muscles twitched?"

"Something like that. He'd be blindfolded, then his head put into a silk bag. Someone in the audience would pretend to stab someone else, then hide the knife by giving it to a third native. Silvertongue would put his hand on a volunteer's shoulder and walk through the crowd picking out the murder victim, the murderer, and the one with the knife. The whole time, he never took off the blindfold or the black silk bag."

"He must have had holes cut in the bag," guessed Slocum.

"Nothing of the sort. The volunteer guiding him would tense—he'd seen the entire murder acted out, after all. He'd never even know it, but Silvertongue's sensitive fingers felt the muscles tightening. He was a true marvel."

"Sounds it."

"He even did himself one better. He made a bet once that he could drive blindfolded to a stash of gold. He put the reins of the team in one hand and put his other on his guide's shoulder." Cara laughed. "Silvertongue almost lost his bet. He got himself a drunk who was so relaxed nothing got him nervous."

"He didn't lose the bet, did he?" Slocum said. "He got around it."

"Sure he did. Silvertongue Wyatt was a genius. He upped and got the team driving through the center of town so fast that he scared the drunk out of his wits. *Then* he could feel the differences in muscle tensings. Found the gold, even if he did cause two of the horses to keel over from exhaustion."

"What about the drunk?"

"Became a deacon in the church. Refused to touch another drop of whiskey. He..."

"Never mind," Slocum said. He knew it when Cara started into a tall tale. While the story about this Argentine Murder Mystery and Wyatt sounded like a whopper, he wondered. Something in Cara's eyes told him this might be the gospel truth. "I get the idea."

"You're getting the bug, John. I see it. This is all

mysterious to you, and it attracts you. Does it attract you as much as I do?"

"Not nearly as much," he admitted.

Cara flashed him a broad smile. When she tried, Cara O'Connell could be a lovely woman. Something told him that she could turn ugly in a flash, though.

"You'll help us out?" she asked.

"Sure, but only with the drunks. I don't know enough to do a pitch."

"That'll be a real boon, John. Drunks are our worst problem. They get to making catcalls and badmouthing Mort and distracting the crowd. Hell and damnation, one of them even drank the alcohol Mort used to keep his tapeworms from decaying."

"What?"

"A fact. The drunk staggered up to the stage. Mort was doing a pitch for a physic that ridded your intestines of tapeworms. He'd got some from a packing house in Kansas City for five dollars. This drunk ups and drains the jar. Spit out the tapeworms. Ruined them. Mort decided not to bother replacing them."

"I'll take care of the drunks for you," he assured Cara.

"And tonight, I'll take care of you," she said in a low, seductive voice. Her hands ran over his muscular body, finding all the right spots. Before Slocum knew it, he was responding fully to her. She looked around, saw Mort Thorogoode inside the wagon working on part of his pitch. Billy and Frieda busied themselves removing the old labels and putting on new ones.

"Tonight's a long ways off," Cara said. "Why wait?"

They got far enough from the wagon so the others couldn't hear Cara's passionate moans as they made love.

Afterward, Slocum decided it might not be a bad idea staying with the medicine show past Socorro, maybe all the way into Albuquerque. Maybe. It certainly had its advantages.

9

Slocum tried to get it straight in his head that Socorro was somehow different from Hot Springs or San Augustine or just about any other frontier settlement. The heat was the same. The dust rose off the streets in the same way. The dull, lifeless eyes peering out at them as they rode through the middle of town varied not one iota from the other places they'd been. Slocum wondered how Thorogoode—and Cara—put up with this sameness.

Cara O'Connell had mentioned the thrill of performing in front of an audience, but Slocum doubted that was the entire attraction for the pretty blonde. Performance like an actress, yes; but the bilking, the swindling, the taking of money for worthless remedies had to be an even bigger part of her excitement. Slocum had seen the way her sallow cheeks flushed and her lips turned redder and more appealing with arousal, almost as if she got a sexual pleasure from the act. Her breath came in short, hurried pants, and her stance told how excited she actually was.

That had to be the glue holding her to the medicine

show. She and Thorogoode certainly weren't doing too well together. Slocum had puzzled over their stormy relationship and decided that it was one based on mutual need. Thorogoode needed a lovely assistant to take some of the strain off his pitch, to divert male attention, to hold out the promise to the plainer women in the audience that his potions would make them look as good as Cara.

For Cara's part, she made a great deal of money, Slocum guessed. Her excitement over the mention of the money from the bank robbery in El Paso didn't hide the fact that she thought a few hundred, maybe even a thousand dollars, was slim pickings. He hadn't forgotten her stories of Thorogoode wearing a fancy coat with buttons made out of twenty-dollar gold pieces and a vest with buttons of half-eagles.

"Pennyweighters," he muttered as he stared out at the listless townsfolk. No diamonds to filch in Socorro. How many diamonds did those in Doctor Denton's Marvelous Travelling Medicine Show have, though? Slocum considered looking through their chests and the tiny compartments inside the medicine-show wagon. If he never caught up with Nathan, he'd need a stake, and a diamond or two would give it.

"Don't go gettin' any ideas, Slocum," came Billy's gruff voice. The man's gray eyes were bright and hotter than the sun outside. The pupils had collapsed into black holes hardly larger than a pinprick. Slocum remembered what Cara had said: opium.

A man hopped out of his fool head on dope wasn't likely to know what he was doing. Slocum didn't answer.

"You'll never steal so much as a nickel from us and get away with it. I don't know what you been doin' for a living, but it'll be a cold day in hell before you catch us looking the other way." The words tumbled out like a muddy river over a dam. Slocum sensed more underneath the flow than he saw, but the flow was enough to convince him he'd made a bad enemy in Billy Ferguson.

"Don't intend stealing from friends," Slocum said. He caught hold of the side of the wagon as Thorogoode ran over a rock in the street. Socorro didn't do much in the way of maintaining its roadways. "Just think about duping them." Slocum pointed to the people now gathering behind the wagon. Some pointed, all muttered. The tension mounted and the show Thorogoode put on would be the finale.

"Asshole." With that Billy ducked back inside the wagon. Slocum heard an argument start between Frieda and Billy. He shut it out. With any luck, this would be about the last time he would have to endure this. Slocum had a gut feeling he would find Nathan or Rawlinson here. The trip out to San Augustine had been a distraction; he was back on their trail now.

Even as he considered he might be wrong and that Nathan might have ridden hell-bent for leather all the way north to Santa Fe without so much as stopping, Slocum saw Nails Rawlinson.

The burly man lounged outside a saloon, leaning indolently against a post sorely in need of paint. Slocum started to get back into the wagon and out of sight, but there wasn't enough time. Rawlinson's beady eyes followed the gaudy wagon—and he never gave the slightest indication he saw Slocum. The smithy's full attention was focused on the gaudy sign and maybe Cara O'Connell up in the box with Thorogoode.

Slocum heaved a sigh of thanks for this small bit of luck. He wanted Nathan so bad he could taste it, even through the grit and trail dust that had accumulated in his mouth. Having Rawlinson spooked and rushing off to tell Nathan would only make matters more difficult. Slocum smiled slowly. Everything was playing right into his hand. The bushwhackers were in Socorro, and they didn't know where he was. Maybe Nathan even thought he was dead.

That notion pleased Slocum even more. He wanted

to savor the surprise on Nathan's face when he asked for
the money from the robbery. Slocum sobered when he
realized that there might not be much left. Maybe none
at all. Nathan was a big-spending blowhard. He'd been
staying at the most expensive hotel in Hot Springs. And
he probably gambled poorly. Slocum began cursing. Nathan might have lost all the money by now.

He swung about and went into the wagon. He blinked
for a moment, not understanding what he saw Billy Ferguson doing. Then he figured it out. Ferguson took a
small eye dropper and transferred a clear liquid from a
small, almost empty bottle into a shot glass of whiskey.
With a quick, nervous movement, Billy knocked back
the drink. Frieda's eyes widened when she saw Slocum
watching. She shook her head, warning Slocum to keep
his peace.

Laudanum. Slocum didn't know where he'd heard the
word, but he figured this was all the opium Billy had
left. For an addict to run this low amounted to disaster.
No wonder he was so touchy.

"John," Frieda said too loudly, after Billy had hidden
away the tiny vial of liquid opiate. "We about ready to
start the pitch?"

"Thorogoode's got a spot picked out," Slocum said.
"The crowd will be waiting for us, unless I miss my
guess. We drew a following mighty fast going through
the center of town like that."

"It always works," Frieda said.

"Don't you go talkin' to him," Billy snarled. He cocked
his fist back, but his hand trembled, and Slocum noted
a softening of the man's hard features. The opium was
already taking its toll on his body.

"He be able to work the crowd?" Slocum asked when
Billy slipped to one side and began to snore loudly.

"It'll wear off in an hour. Always does," Frieda said
bitterly. Then she ignored Slocum as if he didnt' exist.
The woman gathered her fortune-telling cards and corked

up the last of Doctor Denton's Miracle Elixir and Hair Restorer.

The wagon came to a halt and Slocum vaulted to the ground. He teetered for a moment, the ground under his feet feeling as if it moved like the wagon had. Then the false sense of motion vanished, and Slocum got to work tending the mules. His two horses whinnied and protested being neglected until after he'd taken care of the long-eared, balky mules, but Slocum knew which had been doing the work and which had been ambling along beside the wagon.

Thorogoode had changed into his fancy cutaway tail suit and tapped the silk top hat smartly. "Step right up, ladies and gentlemen," he began his pitch. Thorogoode unfurled a new banner and began stringing it along the back of the wagon, behind the small stage and over the door leading inside.

A small titter went up in the crowd. A man yelled out, "Hey, Mister, you got the banner upside down!"

Thorogoode stiffened at the criticism but did nothing to turn the banner right side up.

"Sir," Thorogoode said, "any damn fool can read the lettering with it the other way. This is an exercise for brain and eye!"

Slocum hadn't figured Thorogoode to be unable to read. This made the man's pitch all the more exceptional.

"Ladies and gentlemen, I am Doctor Denton!"

"Some doctor," cried a man at the back of the crowd. "He can't even read!"

"Sir, do you know where the heart is?" Thorogoode thumped his chest. "Do you know where the spine is?" He turned and flexed his shoulder muscles so that his spine rippled a bit. "But do you know where your bowels are?"

A murmur went through the crowd. The man at the back pushed forward, his face reddening with anger.

"I asked you a question, sir. Do you know where your

bowels are?" Thorogoode smiled broadly. "I must admit that even I, Doctor Denton, do not know where *anyone's* bowels are, because they move every day!"

The laughter going through the crowd released the mounting tension. Even the heckler began to grin sheepishly. Several others thumped him on the arm, and soon he laughed with the best of them.

Cara came over and said quietly, "He's going to need some help with this crowd. Mort can handle 'em for a while, but the Doctor Denton pitch is longer than the one for Doctor Wong. Some of them will be getting drunk before he's finished. I told him we were too close to the saloon." Cara lithely climbed onto the stage when Thorogoode introduced her as his "gorgeous assistant, Miss Myrna." Cara curtsied and smiled, showing her dimples.

This kept the crowd occupied for another fifteen minutes, but soon even Cara's beauty was not enough for them. Men came and went, going into the saloon and returning fifteen minutes later, with that much more liquor in their bellies. The catcalls started, and Slocum knew it was time for him to put his untested skills to work.

He found one heckler and stood behind him.

"What'd you do, trade a swayback mule for that one?" the heckler shouted, drunkenly taunting Cara. Slocum moved to the side, then slipped so that he was standing to half block the man's view. Before the drunk could say anything, Slocum stomped down hard with his foot and leaned into the man's body.

"Whatcha doing?" the drunk demanded, but Slocum's weight moved him to the edge of the crowd and distracted him from the action on the small stage. Slocum repeated the action and cut the drunk from the crowd just as he would cut a heifer from the herd for branding. A simple turn to one side caused the man to sit down heavily on the wood-plank sidewalk.

"You all right?" Slocum asked. "You look like you could use a drink. Come on. I'll buy."

"You will?" The drunk fought his way to his feet, forgetting all about heckling Cara and Thorogoode. "Course you will. Damn little to repay for your clumsiness." He worked hard on the last word. Slocum guided him toward the saloon. The man went through the doors, but Slocum didn't follow. By the time the drunk figured out that there wasn't anyone there to buy the drinks, he might have forgotten altogether about the medicine show.

Slocum cut out less obnoxious drunks, and Thorogoode kept the pitch running smoothly. Cara flashed him a quick smile, but other than this she didn't break from her prim and proper role as Miss Myrna, the plain middle-aged lady who had partaken of Doctor Denton's Magical Elixir of Youth and had become as she was now. Who would have believed that Miss Myrna was forty-seven years old? demanded Thorogoode.

Slocum wouldn't. But most of the women in the crowd fervently believed it. Or wanted to.

By the time Thorogoode got to the miracle of the soap that seemed to froth forever—with the added inducement of the Mexican "perfume bean"—Cara, Frieda, and Thorogoode were inundated with women thrusting dollar bills at them. Seeing that all was well in hand, Slocum slipped to the edge of the crowd, then walked away quietly.

He had Nathan and Rawlinson to find. That score needed settling more than Thorogoode needed help selling his fake soap.

The saloon nearest the medicine show turned out to have in it only the barkeep, three card players, and the drunk Slocum had got rid of earlier. He started to ask the barkeep if he'd seen Nathan, then stopped. It wouldn't do to give the bushwhacker even a hint that anyone was on his trail. Slocum backed out and continued down the street. By now the sun had dipped below the mountains to the west and a chilly breeze whipped up tiny dust clouds. The second saloon had more patrons bellied up to the bar, but still no sign of Nathan or Rawlinson.

Slocum went out into the street, the back of his neck feeling prickly. He rubbed over it and came away with a handful of grit, but it wasn't the trail dust that bothered him. He had spent most of his life tracking game. Some of that time had been spent being stalked.

Slocum had the gut-level feeling someone had him marked out as prey and hunted him down. It couldn't be anyone else but Henry Nathan.

Quick, cold green eyes checked out storefronts along the main street. Most businesses had closed. A thin stream of people walked antlike toward the medicine show. Thorogoode's booming voice echoed throughout the still town now. The pitch man had found his tempo, and Slocum figured there were few people not being held mesmerized by the full, vibrant voice and stage presence.

Slocum saw no indication of anyone openly studying him. He turned and felt the eyes boring into his back. His fingers drummed lightly over the butt of his Colt, but he didn't draw. He kept marching along as if nothing was wrong, as if he didn't have a care in the world. Now and again he'd turn and look behind.

Nothing. There was never anyone tracking him down. All he heard were the mournful whistles of wind through the buildings and Thorogoode's increasingly vehement pitch. Slocum pivoted suddenly and ran down a dark alley. At the end, he spun again, drew his pistol, and waited for someone to silhouette himself at the mouth of the alley.

Nothing. No one. Slocum lowered the hammer on his pistol and returned the weapon to his holster. Whoever trailed him was doing a damn fine job of it. Not for an instant did Slocum mistrust his sixth sense. It had been right more often than not—and being wary kept him alive.

Back in the street, he reversed his path and returned to the saloon. In the short time he'd been playing cat and mouse, Nails Rawlinson had entered. The man swallowed one shot of whiskey after another until Slocum's head spun around and around just watching. That much liquor downed so quickly would have made most men pass out. It only seemed to make the burly smithy more active.

"Where's the girls?" Nails demanded of the barkeep. "You keepin' the best'uns up in the crib? I got money. Lemme at 'em. I'll show 'em what a real man can do."

Slocum had seldom heard Rawlinson say more than a dozen words at a stretch. Now he ran off at the mouth. The whiskey had burned away whatever reticence the man normally showed.

Slocum stepped to one side, peering through the door into the saloon. He wanted to make sure he knew where Nathan was before accosting Rawlinson. A heavily painted woman who looked like she'd been rode hard and put away wet came from a back room. The bartender inclined his head toward Nails Rawlinson. She didn't smile until she came up and put one scrawny hand on the big man's shoulder.

"You got enough left to buy the likes of me a drink?" she asked. Slocum waited. After two more overpriced drinks, the whore getting watered-down liquor and Rawlinson full strength, they staggered into the back room. Rawlinson was drunker than a lord and the whore had trouble supporting his teetering bulk.

Only then did Slocum go into the saloon.

"Rye," he ordered. Slocum made a face as he tasted what he'd got. Whatever it was, Old Overholt had no competition. Slocum turned around and rested his elbows on the bar as he surveyed the room. Most of the men were down to serious drinking. Nowhere did he see Nathan.

And the feeling of being watched grew by the second.

Slocum tried unsuccessfully to spin around and catch sight of the man tracking him. His failure worried Slocum more than anything else. Whoever followed him was better than good; he was damn good. He considered rushing back into the street and seeing if he could take whoever was out there by surprise, then decided against it.

Henry Nathan had never shown such skill. If anything, the man was more likely to barge in with guns blazing.

"You with the medicine show?" the barkeep asked.

Slocum nodded.

"Don't get this much excitement in a month, usually. First they got in, then you folks came in."

"'They?'" asked Slocum.

The barkeep lowered his voice. "Shouldn't talk about them, I suppose. But I thought you knew. The Nathan gang. Two of them."

"No lie?" Slocum held his anger in check. No matter where Nathan went, he advertised his presence. Before anyone knew it, unless he was stopped, Nathan would be back East having dime novels written about him and how big a *desperado* he was. Cold anger rose within Slocum. There were those who did and those who just bragged. He couldn't abide by the braggarts.

Like Henry Nathan.

"One of them's in the back room with Miss Sally."

"A real outlaw. Why's the sheriff lettin' them stay in town?" asked Slocum.

"Ain't got a sheriff right now, and the deputy is out at the Davis place east of here." Answering Slocum's unasked question, "Sheriff got kicked in the head by his horse and keeled over dead almost a month ago. Nobody's got around to namin' a new one yet. Most likely it'll be the deputy, but who can say?"

Slocum filed that away for future use. No sheriff meant Thorogoode wouldn't run into any trouble with licenses and bribes. It also meant that Slocum had a free hand in dealing with Nathan.

A group of rowdy cowhands came in and occupied

the barkeep. Slocum took the opportunity to quietly head for the back rooms. Doors lined the narrow hallway and opened into half a dozen cribs. The first four were empty. The fifth was being used, but not by Nails Rawlinson and the whore who'd led him out of the main saloon.

"Sorry," he said. Slocum tipped his hat and quickly shut the door. Only one room left. From inside came the sounds of an elk in rut. Slocum almost smiled. It had to be Rawlinson in there. He slipped his ebony-handled Colt from his holster, cocked the pistol, and slowly opened the door.

The only light came from a small window looking out into the street and a guttering wax candle on a table near the bed. It took Slocum several seconds to figure out the moving silhouettes on the wall. He found the bed and pointed his gun straight down at the moving, hairy ass jutting up in the air.

"Enjoying yourself, Nails?"

Rawlinson thought it was Nathan. At first. The giant of a man rolled off the whore and bellowed, "You leave me the hell alone, Henry. I put up with your..." His voice trailed off when he found himself staring down the barrel of Slocum's pistol.

"Putting my share of the money to good use. A shame you and Nathan didn't see fit to let me decide how I wanted it spent."

"Slocum, see here, it wasn't my fault!" The man fumbled, pulling up the tattered Army blanket on the bed in a vain attempt to hide his nakedness.

"What's going on?" demanded the woman. She sensed how quickly Rawlinson had become sober. "Who are you, bargin' in here like this? I got my rights!"

"We've got business to talk, Nails and I do," said Slocum. "Why don't you just get your clothes back on and go find another customer?"

"Like hell I will!" she raged. "This bastard's not paid me yet!"

"Didn't do much. Shouldn't pay much," observed Slocum, enjoying Rawlinson's discomfort. His gun never wavered. He had it sighted in right between the man's beady eyes.

"Not only didn't he do much, he doesn't have much to do it with," complained the skinny whore. "But he took up my time. That's worth—"

Slocum cut her off. "Here's a half-eagle. That ought to more'n pay you for the time spent." Slocum had rummaged through Rawlinson's trousers and found the coin. A small roll of greenbacks was the only other money he found. Rawlinson licked his lips and stared at the scrip.

"What you planning on doing, Slocum?"

"That's a good question. This isn't anywhere near all the money due me," Slocum said. "It isn't even my cut before Larouche was eliminated from the split." Again the nervous gestures. Rawlinson sweated like a pig now, the perspiration running down his body in rivers.

"That wasn't none of my doing. Honest."

"Honest? You? Hardly. You went along with Nathan."

At mention of Henry Nathan, the whore stopped dressing and looked hard at Slocum, eyes squinting in the dimness. "You one of the Nathan gang?" Awe tinged her words.

"Let's just say I'm collecting on a debt owed me for too long," Slocum said. To Rawlinson he said, "Where's Nathan holed up?"

"He's got the rest of the money. H-he said he'd keep it safe for me."

"Nathan? Where?" Slocum straightened his elbow and made a show of aiming the gun.

"Slocum, believe me, I didn't know he was going to shoot you down like that. I . . ."

The roaring gunshot deafened Slocum. For a second he thought his Colt had fired accidentally, then realized the shot had been fired through the small window at the corner of the room. Slocum spun and saw a dark shadow fluttering away. He was too late to even glimpse who'd gunned down Nails Rawlinson.

By the time the ringing sound of the shot had died in Slocum's ears, the whore's screams had replaced it. Heavy footsteps pounded down the narrow hallway, and the room filled with men aiming shotguns in Slocum's direction.

He released the hammer and raised his hands, wondering if one of those twitchy fingers resting on a trigger might contract and send him a new load of buckshot.

10

The bore of the double-barreled shotgun looked big enough for Slocum to stick his entire head into it. The skinny whore kept screaming, and Nails Rawlinson lay sprawled on the bed with a dark hole in his temple. Whoever had shot through the partly opened window had either been lucky or good. Rawlinson had died in one convulsive jerk. Slocum hadn't been looking forward to the gigantic man challenging the .31 caliber Colt. As good as the Colt Navy was, it didn't have much stopping power when it came to a man that big.

"He did it, he did it," the prostitute babbled. She pointed a bony, accusing finger at Slocum. "He busted in on us and pulled his gun and threatened him." Her watery eyes drifted over to Rawlinson's corpse sprawled naked across the bed. "I got his damned blood on my bed!" she screamed.

Slocum saw the darting glance to Rawlinson's clothes, then to the wad of bills Slocum still held in his left hand. The whore licked her lips. Slocum wished he could get a few seconds alone with Miss Sally. The money would more than change her story. But rough hands grabbed the scrip and held it aloft.

"See here?" demanded the barkeep, the shotgun never wavering. "He robbed that poor jackass. Shot him dead and robbed him!"

"Lynch the bastard!" "Son of a bitch killed him while he was in bed fuckin' Miss Sally." "One of them bank robbers." "Lynch the bastard!"

The voices rose to deafening pitch. Slocum wondered if they would listen to reason. Most mobs heated up for a lynching didn't, and this one was turning uglier by the instant. Now Slocum wished that the sheriff hadn't been kicked in the head and died and that the deputy waiting to be the sheriff wasn't off somewhere. They might not have stopped a lynching, but they'd have slowed it down a mite.

Slocum could already feel the itchy rope around his neck.

He glanced over toward the window where the shot had come from, and decided he'd never reach it, even though it was less than two paces away. The barkeep's beady eyes never left him. The slightest hint of escape would send both barrels of 00 buck into his chest.

"Check my gun," Slocum said. "Never fired. All the chambers are loaded. Check it, damn it!"

"He shot him dead," the whore moaned. The rumble of sentiment rode with Miss Sally. They wanted some more entertainment, and it had probably been a good long time since anyone had been lynched.

Slocum felt hands fumbling at his gun. He heard the cylinder being opened.

"One shot gone," came the verdict.

"I always rest the hammer on an empty. Check the barrel. That gun's not been fired in—"

Slocum crashed back into the wall and slid down, blood spurting from a cut on his cheek where the butt of the shotgun struck him.

"Shut up," ordered the barkeep. "You killed a customer and now you got to pay for it. Somebody get a rope!"

"You folks really know how to make a stranger feel welcome," muttered Slocum. If it had been Nathan who'd shot Rawlinson, all the bank robber's worries were over. He'd gotten rid of Larouche earlier. Now he had the money all to himself once Slocum's feet kicked free, a rope around his neck.

The room was too crowded for Slocum to do anything. The men jammed in and prevented easy entrance and exit. While they might not be able to keep him from grabbing a gun, once he had it there wasn't a paper dog in hell's chance of Slocum doing anything about it. He couldn't shoot down twenty of them with a single gun. They dragged him to his feet and shoved him into the narrow hall. Even here, the spectators crowded in and prevented Slocum from making an escape.

"Who's gonna pay me?" the whore complained. "That bastard shoots down my . . . friend and I get left with bloody sheets and a dead body! And I don't get paid!"

"Poor Sally," said one man, barely able to contain his laughter. "First john she gets all month long, and he gets gunned down while he's on top of her."

Slocum jockeyed for position, ready to sprint when they got to the main room of the saloon, but again his chance for escape was thwarted. Fifty or more men crowded the doorway. Even if he did get away from the shotgun rammed into his spine, there wasn't anywhere to run. The windows were packed with the curious onlookers and the back door to the saloon had been securely bolted.

"Take him to the jail, then get the gallows ready," someone cried out. This was met with universal approval—except on Slocum's part.

"Dig that bullet from his skull. It's not the same caliber. Whoever shot Rawlinson used a .44, from the sound of it."

"He did know him!" shouted another in the crowd. "Think he's one of the Nathan gang?"

"Maybe they had a falling out. If he is, we got two reasons to string him up!"

Whatever Nathan had done or said, it hadn't set well with the people of Socorro. This sleepy, dusty nowhere town had got riled up mighty fast. They were primed and ready for almost anything, even a hanging. *Especially* a hanging.

Slocum was pushed and kicked through the streets of Socorro until they arrived at the jail. The one-story beige adobe structure had seen better days, but the old sheriff had kept the two cells as escape-proof as possible for a small town. Slocum heaved a sigh as the barkeep shoved him into one and slammed the door securely shut. At least he was momentarily away from the crowd.

"Look," he said to the barkeep, "we can work something out. If I am one of the Nathan gang, you know there's got to be some money in it for you if I just happened to get away."

"Mister, I'm a God-fearing man. I know my duty." The barkeep raised the shotgun and pointed it through the bars directly at Slocum. Slocum straightened, but his green eyes never wavered. They locked firmly with the barkeep's softer brown eyes. "Can't let you go," the man said, lowering the shotgun. "You killed a man."

"Even if that was true—and it isn't—how's lynching me do anything for you?"

"Keeps you from doing it again."

"You got my word I'll ride out of here and never come back."

"And kill somewhere else? No, mister, this keeps you from slaughtering innocent men and women everywhere."

"Can't argue with that, even though I didn't kill Rawlinson. Someone shot him through the window."

The barkeep snorted and said nothing. He began nervously pacing the small office, peering out into the street as he waited for a rope to be knotted and a proper sized crowd to gather. Most everyone in Socorro would want to witness a hanging. Anyone left out would be fit to be tied.

Slocum did some pacing of his own, but he didn't get very far in any direction. The front of the cell was securely barred even though the black paint had been scraped off the iron. Getting through the door would take a stick of dynamite. The thick adobe back wall, with a tiny barred window set in it up at eye level, would take weeks of digging to get through. Slocum's life span was being measured in minutes. One wall led to the other cell; no gain there. The final wall was probably as thick as the back, and maybe thicker since it faced to the south.

Even though the adobe kept it cool inside the jail, Slocum was quickly drenched in sweat. He'd gone through the War, ridden with Quantrill, survived hell during Reconstruction, and now ended up in a New Mexico Territory jail getting ready to be hanged. He couldn't even call Socorro a backwater town—there wasn't enough water for that.

"They got the gallows ready," said the barkeep. "They're coming for you."

"I can wait," muttered Slocum.

A dozen men, guns drawn, burst into the tiny jail and took Slocum out. He lost sight of the barkeep in the wild swirl of the crowd. Even the womenfolk had gathered for the hanging. This was a bigger show than even Doctor Denton's Marvelous Travelling Medicine Show.

Hands tied behind him, they pulled Slocum up the gallows steps. He wondered that they had a gallows already constructed but lacking a rope. Might have been a few months since it was used, and the rope had been put to better use than simply dangling in the hot sun.

Whatever that rope had been used for, Slocum wished it had stayed there.

"On the trap. Stand on the trap," one of the lynch mob ordered.

A small commotion started at the back of the crowd and moved forward. Slocum watched in fascination. It looked like a duck swimming on a still pond, leaving ripples behind. Mort Thorogoode, dressed up in his Doctor Denton outfit, mounted the thirteen steps to stand on the gallows not three feet away. Their eyes met for the briefest of instants.

Slocum dared to hope.

The man to his right stood with the noose in his hand, but his attention had shifted to Thorogoode. The others on the gallows were similarly taken with Thorogoode's pose and commanding air. The talent of selling phony patent medicines now turned to saving John Slocum. Why he would bother, Slocum couldn't say, but he wasn't going to argue the point.

"Ladies and gentlemen," Thorogoode said, immediately quieting the restive crowd. "I have come to make an offer which might sound implausible to you, but which can be of immeasurable gain for all of society."

"Get on with the hanging," someone in the center of the crowd grumbled. Others near him silenced the outcry.

"We got a hanging to do, Doc," the man with the noose said. "Why don't you just let us get on with it?"

"Let him have his say, Clem," another said. "We ain't in no hurry."

Slocum was happy to hear that.

"Society neither applauds nor condemns your action this day," Thorogoode went on, as if he hadn't heard any of the comments. "But it is to your children, yes, those babes in arms today, to whom you owe this sterling opportunity. I have travelled the length and breadth of this great land seeking out a cure for criminal tendencies."

"You mean," cut in one of the men on the gallows, "you can give this owlhoot a swig of medicine and cure him?" The skepticism of the crowd was obvious. Thorogoode chose not to contradict.

"Nothing of the sort," he said smoothly. "But I *search* for such a potion. Imagine the day, ladies and gentlemen, when our most vicious criminals, our deadliest killers"— he looked over his shoulder at Slocum—"can be cured of their tendencies by a simple Elixir of Criminal Proclivity Eradication."

Thorogoode lowered his voice and stilled any protests. All the people hung on his every word. "I am close, dear citizens of Socorro, so very close. But I am not yet there!"

"So hang the bastard!" came the outcry.

"No!" Thorogoode's hand shot upward and silenced them effectively. "But I am close, very close. Can you deny me the chance I need to examine this man's brain to find those parts that have withered or become leprous with criminal lesions?"

"What are you saying?"

"I must cut open this man's umbilicus and operate on his tweedlum. Only in this way can I find the curative potion that will prevent others from becoming purveyors of criminality!"

Slocum took his cue when Thorogoode nodded slightly. He shouted at the top of his lungs, "You can't do that! It's too cruel! Hang me instead. Don't let him take out my . . . my . . ." Slocum couldn't remember what Thorogoode had said.

Thorogoode's hand silenced Slocum. "Perhaps the poor, perverted man is right. Even for such a hardened criminal, my techniques now might be considered too brutal. Yes, go on, hang him. Get it over with. My criminal cure must wait for another day."

That put the cap on it. The women in the crowd began muttering to let the good doctor have him, especially if it meant the difference between success and failure in finding this marvelous cure. After all, hadn't Doctor Denton introduced them to the wonder of his soap? And what of the Mexican perfume bean? One or two even had the nerve to mention the youth restoring potion. Surely, any man capable of developing such a boon to humanity could find a cure for criminal behavior.

The men in the lynch mob weren't so certain. They knew hanging and that was what they'd had their hearts set on. But Thorogoode's suasions carried the day.

"To my wagon!" Thorogoode cried. "There is no time to waste. I must operate immediately!"

If anything, the crowd grew in size. Slocum worried as to what Thorogoode would do next. The man's sallow complexion was all the more apparent in the torchlight as they rushed to the other end of town. Whatever happened, though, Slocum had been given a reprieve. If the chance presented itself, and he figured Thorogoode had something of the sort in mind, he'd get on his horse and ride like the wind. There was no way in hell he would ever be able to convince anyone in Socorro that he hadn't killed Nails Rawlinson.

It galled Slocum to think that Nathan might get away scot free, but he had more immediate worries.

"My assistant, Miss Myrna, has already set up the operating table. This will be a delicate operation. I must ask you to stand back and give me room. Except for you, sir; if you'd be so kind as to stand right there and hold the torch. Thank you. You are helping the cause of Natural Science."

Thorogoode positioned the one man at the far right edge of the narrow stage on the back of the wagon. Slocum worried that the man was still too close, but Thorogoode had his reasons for positioning everyone where they were.

"Just lie down and moan," Cara said softly. Slocum laid on the simple plank table, and Cara covered him with a dirty muslin sheet. Her hand fumbled under the sheet; he felt a sharp knife slicing through the ropes binding his hands.

He looked up into her eyes. She smiled slightly. A cold steel rod rammed into his hands. It took Slocum several seconds to realize that she had given him back his gun. How or where Cara had recovered it, he didn't know. But he was armed again, and ready for whatever had to be done.

Frieda helped Thorogoode into a white smock. The man stood with a shining cleaver in his hand. He turned it from side to side so that it caught and reflected the light from the guttering torch. The torch holder swallowed hard and looked as if he might get sick to his stomach.

"There, sir, hold the light steady. I must not make a mistake at this critical instant." Thorogoode looked down at Slocum. In a voice too low for anyone else to overhear, he said, "Don't move. If you do, you'll lose your head."

Thorogoode did something that Slocum couldn't see. Then another white sheet was draped over his face, completely covering his head. Through the cloth Slocum saw the dim, moving shadows. Thorogoode's hand clutching the cleaver rose, then came hurtling down.

A solid *thunk!* on the table just above Slocum's head produced gasps from the crowd. He even heard one or two begin to retch. Wetness flowed around his head and neck and along his shoulders. Slocum didn't stir. Whatever Thorogoode had moved under the cloth at the last instant had been neatly severed, and the crowd thought it was the top of his head.

"There is the culprit," came Thorogoode's satisfied words. "This gray tumor is responsible for the poor wight's behavior. I must put this into a bottle and study it further, to find the proper medicines to reduce it in size and even to eliminate it. Yes, ladies and gentlemen, we have this very day seen a breakthrough in Natural Science."

"What about him?" came the question.

"This demented murderer? Alas, there is nothing we can do for him. He has made his contribution to science.

But if you would permit me one further liberty, I can use his bodily parts for other experiments. None so noble as the prevention of criminal activity, perhaps, but I might find some clue as to curing diarrhea and dropsy and ague and other maladies."

"Give him the body," came the choked words. "What do we want with it? Just another grave out in the potter's field we don't have to dig."

"You want the other one's body? The one he murdered?"

Thorogoode seemed taken aback by this suggestion, but he recovered nicely. "No, not at all. He has passed beyond the vale too long ago. Only the most recently dead are of any use to me."

Slocum heard the crowd muttering and beginning to disperse. They had had a busy day. Doctor Denton's Miraculous Travelling Medicine Show, a murder, almost a lynching, and, topping it all off, a scientific experiment.

Then someone jerked away the sheet and saw that Slocum's head still rested firmly attached to his shoulders.

"He's not dead!" the man with the torch shouted. "They tricked us!"

Slocum hesitated for an instant, and found the man jumping up on the table to pin him down. Slocum's Colt discharged, the bullet winging its way over the heads of those in the crowd. Many ran. Others came back. Their chance for seeing a hanging had just multiplied into the possibility of several hangings.

Slocum heaved and tossed the man off. He fell heavily into the dust at the back of the wagon. Slocum sat up on the operating table and pointed his gun at the crowd. He saw instantly how futile this was. They outnumbered him twenty to one.

"He's been resurrected!" shouted Thorogoode. "My God, he must have taken some of my miracle restorative before the operation! Why didn't anyone tell me?"

Slocum pointed the gun at Thorogoode, then saw this wouldn't slow down the crowd. They were turning ugly again. They wanted a lynching.

On impulse, Slocum swung off the table and whirled around, sticking the gun to Cara O'Connell's head. "Don't worry," he whispered. "This might get us all out of here."

Slocum shouted, "Stand back or the lady gets a bullet through her head."

The mob halted, indecisive, until someone said, "That's all right. The doc here can restore her. Ain't that what happened with the killer?"

"No, no, I can't restore life to the dead," Thorogoode shouted, but he had lost control of the crowd. They no longer listened to him or his improbable stories of medical science. And Slocum saw that Cara's life meant nothing to them, either. They had been cheated out of a hanging before, but not now. It would take a hell of a lot more than the threat of another murder to stop them. If anything, his shooting down Cara would only add to the angry crowd's resolve. He'd be a two-time murderer being punished.

"Is everything ready to get out of town?" Slocum asked Thorogoode. The phony doctor nodded, even as he pressed himself against the door leading into the wagon.

"It's not going to do us any good. We can't outrun all of them. Not when we're being pulled by a team of goddamn mules."

Slocum heard Billy up in the box. The man was ready to go, but what Thorogoode said was right. How could they outrun a mob?

Unless the lynch mob decided not to follow.

An idea came to Slocum. He shoved Thorogoode into a few men clambering onto the stage. To Cara he said, "Make it sound convincing."

"What?" she asked, but Slocum was already moving into action with lightning swiftness. He grabbed the first bottle he found on the rack just inside the wagon door.

Pale brown liquid sloshed in the half-filled clear glass bottle.

Slocum held the bottle up high and put the gun to it. "Come any closer and I'll fire!" He nudged Cara to respond. For a heart-stopping moment, he thought she wasn't going to say anything. Then she got her wits about her.

"Watch out!" she screamed. "That's a bottle of diphtheria!"

"What?" The leader of the mob hesitated now, halfway up onto the stage. His eyes went up to the brown liquid. "Diphtheria?"

"Doctor Denton has been doing experiments with it. That bottle will give everyone who comes into contact with it a terrible case of diphtheria. Do as he says!"

"Like hell we will!" The mob turned angry and surged forward again, but the explosion of breaking glass as Slocum fired a round through the bottom of the bottle not only halted the advance but set them back. Men began muttering. Many near the stage had been splashed with the liquid. Slocum himself winced. He'd been cut some by the flying glass, and whatever the potent liquid was, it burned like a house afire wherever it touched his skin.

"Diphtheria!" screeched one man. He turned and bolted into the night. "I'm dying of diphtheria!"

That broke the nerve of the mob. Only a few were left, and they, too, started backing away. When they ran, Slocum relaxed a mite.

"Billy, get us out of here! They're going to think of burning us out before too long." The wagon creaked and protested and the mules brayed, then Doctor Denton's Miraculous Travelling Medicine Show started away from Socorro.

Slocum kicked what was left on the stage off and collapsed just inside the door, his pistol resting across his lap. He looked up when Cara came to him and began wiping away the brown liquid.

"What is that stuff? Not really diphtheria, is it?"

"No, just some of the oil of capsicum. It's harmless enough. And you were magnificent." She kissed him soundly.

"Should be thanking Thorogoode. He saved my neck from getting stretched. Why'd he do it, anyway? There's no love lost between us, and I'm not sure I'd've done the same for him."

Cara stared back at Socorro. "He owed it to you," she said.

"What do you mean by that?"

The woman rose silently and went back inside the wagon to join Thorogoode and Frieda Ferguson. Slocum hadn't got an answer. But he would.

11

Slocum thought Billy Ferguson would turn the wagon over in the dark, but the man seemed to have an angel on his shoulder guiding him through the night. Slocum saw that the horse he'd taken after Larouche had been killed in Hot Springs was missing. His own labored to keep up with the wagon, even though the mules couldn't pull that fast. He sighed. The world turned to ash around him.

The one chance he had had of finding Henry Nathan lay dead back in Socorro, a heavy bullet through his temple. Slocum had almost been lynched. For all he knew, a horde of crazed citizens now formed a posse to come after them, though he doubted that.

Slocum had to smile at the peppery oil that was making his clothes stink. "Diphtheria," he said aloud. Then he began to laugh. So what if he was out the money, that he had scant chance of tracking down Nathan now, that he'd better never show his face in Socorro again? So what? He was still alive.

"What's so funny, John?" Cara asked him.

He dropped into a cross-legged sitting pose on the floor and stared up at the woman. Thorogoode had collapsed on one of the bunks; his chest rose and fell in a thready, strained manner. Slocum had to wonder if the excitement hadn't physically harmed "Doctor Denton."

"Just thinking how life's turned to shit around me," he said. "Nothing's gone right since I was foolish enough to help Nathan with his bank robbing."

"That's funny? You're a strange one," she said. Frieda Ferguson had gone to sleep, or at least feigned sleep, and Billy worked the reins with his shoulders hunched forward, as if to distance himself from those inside the wagon.

"Wasn't meant to have any of the money, I reckon," he told her. "The harder I try, the closer I get to it, the more trouble I find. Still, there's a lot of temptation to keep looking." Deep down, Slocum wasn't going to forget what Nathan had done. After all he'd been through, Slocum would go to the ends of the earth to track down Nathan. To hell with the money from the bank. He *owed* that son of a bitch.

Nobody bushwhacked John Slocum and lived to brag on it.

"Mostly," Slocum said, "I was thinking about the people back there in Socorro. How long before they figure out they don't have diphtheria?"

"What's the difference? A year from now, if anyone comes down with it, you'll be blamed." Cara had to smile, too. "It was funny, the look on that man's face when he got the oil of capiscum all over him. He looked like he'd heard somebody walking on his grave."

"Why'd Thorogoode rescue me?" Slocum asked. Cara couldn't run this time. She turned away and placed one hand on Thorogoode's forehead. The man stirred. Slocum saw that he was drenched in heavy sweat, obviously not a well man. "He needs some of his own medicine."

"You're right. And we don't have any that'll help him. We'll have to get it when we reach New Albuquerque."

"Stores sell what you need? Can't say I ever looked around much for such things."

"Rumors have it that Cosmopolitan Drugstore has the . . . what Mort needs."

"Do folks in the medicine shows trade recipes, where to get the ingredients, things like that?"

"You make us sound like a sewing circle of old women trading recipes," the blonde woman said. "But we do trade some information. If the Cosmopolitan Drugstore doesn't have our supplies, W. Y. Walton's does. Learned that from old Doc Grant when we ran into him out in Oakland last year."

"You do get around," Slocum said.

He realized that Cara had turned the topic away from why Thorogoode had rescued him. He settled back and considered. Maybe a lump of goodness resided somewhere in the bogus doctor's breast, and he was just doing what he saw as his duty. Slocum didn't like that explanation, because it hardly fit Mort Thorogoode, but stranger things had happened.

"We'll be in New Albuquerque in another few days. Then we can find someplace more . . . private," Cara promised. "I want to pay you back for all you've done. In a special way." Slocum found his breathing coming faster, just listening to the way Cara spoke. It wasn't so much the words or the promise as the way she said it. She had Thorogoode's gift for swaying emotions, too, and she turned it on full now. He figured that men had killed to get a fraction as much promise from Cara O'Connell as he now received.

"Think you can stand being with a man almost lynched for being a murderer?"

Her reaction startled him. She stiffened and turned away.

"I didn't kill Rawlinson," he said. "I thought you knew that."

"I do."

Cara refused to say anything more. Slocum stretched out on the floor, found a blanket to use as a pillow, and drifted off to a fitful sleep in the bouncing wagon. Whatever was disturbing Cara, he'd find out about it. But later. Now all he wanted to do was sleep.

"We have to find the marshal and see about licenses," Cara declared. Billy Ferguson and Thorogoode had spent most of their time the past two days in the back of the wagon asleep. Slocum had taken over the chore of driving, though he hardly thought of it that way. He preferred being in the box, watching the barren terrain pass slowly by, being in a position where he could see what was happening.

For the three days up the Rio Grande from Socorro to Albuquerque, he had worried about pursuit. He finally decided that the threat of diphtheria was stronger than the desire for vengeance in the good citizens of Socorro. What was Nails Rawlinson to the people of Socorro, anyway? He was just another wanted outlaw who'd finally come to the end of his trail. The only one probably still angry over it would be the whore, and even she might have come out of it all right. The notoriety of having a wanted outlaw gunned down in her bed might make her more interesting to a certain type of man.

Slocum wondered if she had ever got her sheets cleaned. Probably not.

"This where we're setting up?" Slocum asked. They had followed Railroad Avenue through the center of the town, past Fourth and on toward the mountains to the east. He hadn't missed the obvious slum area a few blocks to the south on Copper, nor had he failed to see the Chinese scurrying about. There weren't many, but more than Slocum would have thought for a town this far from San Francisco.

"They came in when the railroad was built. Just stayed," Cara told him when she saw his interest. "Not too many of them, from all that I've heard. Thirty or less."

"The rail's built. What do they do?"

"Laundry, waiters, jobs like that. Albuquerque's not big enough for many people, much less their kind."

Slocum looked at Cara, startled at the bitterness in her words.

"What is 'their kind?'" he asked.

Cara ignored him, pointing. "There. We can set up there. We're far enough from the plaza to satisfy the merchants there that we're not crowding in on their business, but close enough in so's people will flock around once we start. God, I get tired of these jerkwater towns."

"Want to go back to San Francisco?"

The dreamy look she got in her eye and the way the color rushed to her pale cheeks told Slocum that he'd hit on Cara O'Connell's secret dream. If he told her he had recovered the money from the bank robbery and that he would take her to San Francisco, she'd follow him anywhere.

Something churned inside Slocum. He wasn't sure he wanted the woman on terms like those. Not Cara, not any woman. Slocum didn't look at himself as a meal ticket or a way out. There had to be more.

With Cara O'Connell there was more, but he'd never figured out exactly what it was. Secrets and Cara seemed to go hand in hand.

"The marshal's office is back there a ways," she said, indicating the direction from which they'd come. "I've heard it's a good thing for two of us to ask for it. Especially a man. Not like some towns." The grim expression on her face told Slocum what she'd had to do in some places to get a working license.

Slocum tended to the mules and Frieda began setting up the banners and taking care of the chores required for the show. Her husband and Mort Thorogoode still slept inside the wagon. Slocum thought they must be closer to death than life to sleep through the stifling desert heat and the bouncing of the wagon. He stretched his arms and arched his back to get blood back into joints cramped from staying in one position too long. A breeze drifted through the sleepy streets and evaporated the sweat instantly, giving a cool sensation that made him shiver a mite.

That was the way it always worked in the desert. A man might die from lack of water, but if he sweated enough he'd feel cool as he slipped away.

"Frieda can do what's needed," Cara said. "Let's hurry and get this over with."

"What's the rush? It'll be another four or five hours before dusk. I heard Mort say he didn't want to get started till then. Cooler. Didn't figure the natives would come out in the sun." Slocum smiled to himself. He had fallen into medicine-show slang and had called the locals "natives" and had hardly noticed.

"No rush," Cara said in such a way that Slocum knew she was lying. But she refused to say another word.

They walked back along Railroad Avenue in silence. Slocum's quick eyes darted from side to side, not missing an alleyway or store, the people in and on the street, the possibilities. The faster-travelling Henry Nathan ought to have made it to Albuquerque by now. Slocum fingered the ebony butt of his Colt Navy. Nthan had much to answer for.

"There," Cara said. "There's the marshal's office."

For a moment Slocum failed to spot it; then he saw a single doorway on a storefront next to the office of the *Albuquerque Daily Citizen*. The paint had peeled off the sign and only those actively seeking it could have figured that this was the marshal's office.

Slocum turned to Cara and saw her weave slightly. He put an arm around her shoulders and supported her. "Are you all right? Too much sun?" he asked, concerned.

Cara's face had turned paler than a bleached sheet and her eyes blurred into unfocused pools of green. He led her over to the front of a saloon where chairs had been placed for patrons wanting to enjoy the sights of the city streets. Under a sign proudly proclaiming, LIQUOR IN FRONT, POKER IN THE REAR he settled Cara down.

"Just a touch of sunstroke," the woman said, but Slocum knew otherwise. The burning in the cheeks, the unnatural white of her skin, the suddenly intense expression were not those of someone out in the sun too long. "John, go on and talk to the marshal. I . . . I'll wait here."

"Let me get you some water."

"Never mind," Cara said, trying to smile. The way her lips pulled back made it into a feral snarl. "I'll be just fine if I can sit for a minute or two." She pressed a small pouch into his hands. Slocum peered inside and saw the sharp glint of gold coins.

Slocum nodded and went into the marshal's office. The man was as skinny as a rail and looked meaner than a coyote with its tail stepped on. It only took Slocum a few seconds to find the right bribe. For twenty dollars Doctor Denton's Marvelous Travelling Medicine Show could perform for two days. And the marshal made it known that he'd expect a small bonus if business was brisk—and maybe if it wasn't.

Slocum quickly left with the scribbled-on piece of paper in his hand. Not much of a license, but it would do. He looked across to where he'd left Cara. Slocum wasn't surprised to find the woman gone. The midday heat kept most people indoors or quietly taking a *siesta* in what shade they could find. That made the dark movement down the street all the more apparent.

Slocum started after Billy Ferguson.

Ferguson walked briskly away from the store. Slocum took a quick look inside Ruppe's Cosmopolitan Drugstore window as he passed and saw the usual variety of potions and remedies. Most of them could have been concocted in the back of Thorogoode's wagon. The Great Turkish Rheumatic Cure, the porcelain leech jars, Simmon's Liver Regulator, Dr. Pierce's Pleasant Pellets, the odd implements of the business, the advertisements for Hood's and Ayer's sarsaparillas.

Slocum knew Billy Ferguson might have only been inside shopping for the raw materials Thorogoode used. Slocum remembered Cara mentioning this particular store as being one of the suppliers. But something didn't strike Slocum as being right. The furtive way Billy sneaked out told Slocum there had to be more.

He followed Ferguson and lost him when the man made a quick turn into an alley. Slocum stood and scratched his head. He was an expert tracker, but he'd lost Billy Ferguson in the blink of an eye. He slowly went down the alleyway and came out at the corner of Third and Copper.

Just a couple of blocks made a big difference. Slocum felt unseen eyes studying him from all quarters. The low adobe buildings all had small windows with curtains pulled against the day's heat, but the watchers had to be peering out at him. Slocum walked along briskly, taking in every detail. The faint smell of roasting peanuts reached his nostrils. This was one of the last odors he'd have expected in Albuquerque. He remembered with some fondness the goober peas back in Georgia, how the family had gathered and made a celebration out of toasting a sackful.

Lost in the memories, Slocum almost failed to react when the shadow of a gun fell across the wall to his right. He jerked forward and spun. The butt of the descending pistol missed the top of his head and glanced off his shoulder. It numbed it a mite, but he was able to swing around and drive his fist hard into the exposed belly behind him.

Billy Ferguson grunted and staggered back a pace. Slocum gave him no chance to recover. He grabbed the man's right wrist and forced the muzzle of the gun up and away. A hard knee to the groin doubled Billy up again. Slocum pinned the man against a dried mud brick wall like a butterfly in a collection.

"Got any reasons why I shouldn't just go on and finish what you started?" Slocum asked. He twisted and forced Billy to drop the pistol. Slocum's other hand clamped firmly on Billy's neck. The man's complexion had returned to a normal ruddiness, and the bright shininess of his eyes reflected only hatred.

"Go to hell!" Billy spat.

"Sometimes I think I'm already there. Why'd you try to ambush me?"

"Hell, I missed the other time. Why shouldn't I try again?"

"The other time?" Slocum frowned. Billy hadn't had his pistol with him when Slocum had stopped the man from beating up his wife.

"In Socorro. Damn light was poor. Thought that was you in bed with the whore."

"You killed Rawlinson?" Everything snapped into crystal clarity. Bily had been following him and had tried to gun him down, and had got Nails Rawlinson instead. "Didn't much matter to you, then, when they tried to lynch me."

"That would have been even better!" The man shouted. Slocum quieted him with increased pressure on his windpipe. Billy gurgled a bit and struggled, but Slocum held him too tight.

"Wife-beating and backshooting," Slocum said. "You surely are one piss-poor example of manhood."

Billy tried to spit in his face, but Slocum tensed and lifted. Billy's feet left the dusty sidewalk, and both of the man's hands clawed at Slocum's wrist in a futile attempt to pry loose the strangling fingers.

"I'm going to finish what I started out there in the desert. Never did hold with woman-beating." Slocum whirled and heaved. Billy went tumbling into the dust.

Slocum whirled and heaved. Billy went tumbling into the dust. Slocum caught the man in the ribs with the toe of his boot and sent him rolling. Another kick to the chin snapped Billy's head back and glazed his eyes. Slocum picked him up by the front of his shirt, steadied him, and then drove a hard fist wrist-deep into the man's belly. Billy doubled over so that Slocum could lift a knee into his chin.

Slocum had broken out into a cold sweat now. he got to liking Billy less and less as all his frustrations boiled to the surface. Billy Ferguson became a substitute for Nathan and the others who had screwed him over in the past few weeks. The starving on the trail, the lack of jobs, the bank robbery and bushwhacking, the hardships along the way—it all came out.

Slocum swung and connected firmly with the side of Billy's head, sending the man back to the ground.

"Get up so I can hit you again," Slocum said. "I haven't even begun to show you what I think about you and your weasel ways."

Billy rose to hands and knees, head dangling. Blood dribbled out of his nose and into the thirsty dust. To Slocum's surprise, the man managed to get to his feet again. Ferguson showed little sign of pain as Slocum decked him once more.

"You're not going to wear me out. I promise you that." Slocum saw Billy furtively looking over to where his pistol lay in the dust. Slocum smiled slowly. "I'd like you to try for the gun. I really would." Slocum's face lost all expression, and for the first time Billy showed real fear. He read the killer in Slocum and knew he'd crossed the wrong man.

"Don't gun me down. Please."

Slocum hated whiners even worse than bushwhackers. Both were cowards, but the whiners tried to get out of the consequences of their deeds.

"John, wait, no, don't do it!" Cara O'Connell's voice

stopped Slocum from pulling his Colt and putting a lead-bored hole through Billy's head. Instead, as Billy went for his lost pistol, Slocum stepped forward and kicked him again. Billy rolled away, whimpering.

Slocum turned to Cara, keeping one eye on Billy to make sure he didn't try anything more than sobbing quietly to himself. "Where did you go?" Slocum demanded.

"I . . . I felt stronger. I went back to the wagon." Cara's complexion had changed for the better. No longer did she have that gaunt, haunted look about her. The heat had gone from her cheeks and her eyes sparkled now. Almost too much.

Slocum inhaled and found neither sweat nor perfume on the woman's clothing but the lingering odor of roasted peanuts.

"John, please come back to the wagon. I . . . we have to talk. It's very important. Please!"

Slocum cast one last look at Billy. He didn't even bother taking the gun away from the man. If Billy wanted to get another, it would be easy in Albuquerque. This showed how little Slocum feared him. Deep down inside, Slocum didn't think Billy had the guts to do anything more. Twice he'd taken his licks for being stupid. The likes of Billy Ferguson could never summon the courage to try a third time.

"You knew he'd gunned down Rawlinson back in Socorro, didn't you?" Slocum accused.

Cara nodded, biting her lower lip. "Mort knew, too. That's why he tried to get you away from the lynch mob."

"But he wouldn't just turn Billy over to them." Slocum was disgusted with Billy and Cara and Mort Thorogoode and the medicine show. When he got back to the wagon, he'd saddle up his horse and ride on. Santa Fe was only a few days' travel up the river. In a month he could be lost in the Rockies west of Denver, far from such conniving and backshooting. The fur trapping might not be so good this time of year but it would get better in a couple of months. That might set him up for the entire winter in Denver or even St. Louis.

"How could he?" Cara asked. "Billy's one of us. You're an outsider."

"Thorogoode didn't much take to our being together either, did he?"

"Mort doesn't own me!" she flared. "We've been together a goodly while, but he doesn't tell me what to do. He needs me in the show. Whether I'm doing Princess Lotus Blossom or Miss Myrna or some other character, he needs me to help sell to the natives."

Slocum didn't add the rest of it, but it went through his mind: Cara O'Connell needs Mort Thorogoode, too.

"There's the wagon," he said. The horse stood to one side, tethered to a tree where it could crop the sparse grass beneath. He didn't like disturbing the animal after it had travelled so long through the heat, but he would. It would be best for both of them. "I'll be riding on now," he told Cara. "I've had enough of Billy and Thorogoode—and you."

"John, I need you! You can't do this. Mort's in trouble. Bad trouble."

The expression on his face convinced Cara he was unmoved by this. If anything, it only added to his determination to leave.

She broke down and sobbed. "He's so weak, John. He can't help himself."

"What are you talking about?"

"Mort. He . . . he's like Billy. He's addicted to opium. He's gone off to find a hop joint, and it might kill him. It's been so long for him, he might not be able to take it."

"There's nothing I can do about that. If I did find him, he'd only sneak out again when I wasn't looking. I'm not the man's keeper."

"He did try to save you in Socorro."

"If it hadn't been for Billy, there wouldn't have been

any need to save me. And Thorogoode could have turned
Ferguson over to the mob." Even as he said that, Slocum
knew it wasn't right. Whatever their business relationship, he guessed Thorogoode and Billy Ferguson were
also friends. There wasn't any way in hell Thorogoode
could have given Billy over to a lynch mob.

Slocum softened even more when Cara threw her arms
around his neck and buried her face in his shoulder. The
dampness of her tears soaked into his shirt. "He can't
help himself. He can't. Please find him. Just this once."

Slocum wasn't sure exactly what happened. He was
kissing Cara and she was returning the kiss with growing
ardor. And then they were alone in the wagon, wrestling
back and forth on the narrow floor.

"Please, John, help me, help me forget everything,"
Cara pleaded. Her fingers worked on his shirt and gunbelt
and denims and got him to the place where he felt her
naked breasts rubbing across his sweat-slicked chest. The
hard points of her nipples dug in and aroused him even
more. When her nimble fingers dragged forth his throbbing erection, he gasped and closed his eyes for a moment, trying to keep control.

All this had happened too fast, almost in a daze. He
felt Cara's legs opening for him. His hand moved across
her heaving belly, dallied for a few seconds at the deep
depression of her navel, and then slid lower. Crinkly
blonde fur met his fingers, then smooth, moist flesh.
Cara groaned in pleasure. His fingers worked along the
slit he found, smearing the juices leaking out, getting
her ready.

She tugged harder at his length. "In, John. I need you
inside me. Do it now. Do it, ohhhh!"

He levered his hips forward, found where he had
already explored with his fingers, and slid easily into the
woman's steamy, seething interior. He groaned softly at
the pleasure. Tightness all around his length. Moist, warm,
clinging female flesh surrounded him.

Cara locked her heels behind his back and rocked up on her shoulders, pulling him even deeper into her. They both moaned now. He began moving in slow circles, grinding his crotch into her blonde-furred one.

The heat of the desert, the heat of their bodies, the burning heat of their passion rose until Slocum thought he'd been popped into an oven. He was hardly aware of reaching out and gripping the succulent cones of titflesh or catching the hard nipples between his fingers. He rolled the dark pink buds around and was rewarded with Cara's tiny yelps of need.

Her body rose from the wagon floor and demanded more of his. He gave it to her. Sliding back and forth, moving faster and faster, he sank deep into her tight sheath. She tensed and relaxed, squeezing harder and harder on his pounding erection.

If someone had detonated a stick of dynamite in his loins, Slocum wouldn't have felt any different. Together the pair of them rocked to and fro, smashing into the wooden cabinets lining the tiny passageway in the wagon. When their passions were spent, Slocum sank forward and lay full length on the panting woman.

"Oh, John, I need you so. For so many things," Cara said softly. Her fingernails raked lightly along his bare back, traced over the scars, stimulated him anew.

He pushed himself upright and peered down into her eyes. "Where do you think Thorogoode's gotten off to?" he said, disgusted with himself.

"Nowhere he can't wait another few minutes," Cara O'Connell said, pulling Slocum back down on top of her.

12

Slocum hated himself for letting his balls do his thinking, but there was no getting around the fact that he'd agreed to go hunting for Mort Thorogoode.

"Damn you," Slocum said in a barely audible voice as he looked over at Cara O'Connell. The woman made a big play out of changing her clothing. For a few minutes she stood buck naked so that he couldn't miss the show, turning this way and that, giving him tantalizing glimpses of her sleek white body. Cara now dressed simply in a white blouse with a frilly neckline and a dark brown skirt that fell straight to her ankles. But Slocum knew what lay beneath the covering. Cara had been careful to let him see it. All of it.

Louder, Slocum asked, "Where's Thorogoode likely to be? You mentioned the Cosmopolitan Drugstore. I saw Billy Ferguson coming out of there. Can they get their opium there?"

Cara's lascivious smile faded. "There are seven places where Mort might have gone. One is a tent over on

Second Street, not too far from the post office."

"Seven?" Slocum groaned. This was turning into a bigger project than he had anticipated.

"Another's in the Wing Sing Laundry, just west of Fifth." Cara frowned, thinking. "West of Fourth, between Copper and Railroad, in Cuing's place."

"You sure seem to know where they all are," Slocum said suspiciously.

"Mort's got good information. They . . . they all exchange information about where the best opium is to be found. I listen. You never know." Cara looked at him, one eyebrow arched slightly.

"You never know," Slocum agreed.

"Charlie Jew runs one just north of Copper Avenue; another Chinaman—I don't know his name—is supposed to be over near First Street. Then there's Quong down in Old Town."

"That's six," Slocum said, mentally trying to figure where each was from his brief trip through Albuquerque. "I'd guess there ought to be another down near the railroad yards." Cara nodded. "So which one should I start with?"

"I don't know," said the woman. "Any of them. All of them. If I knew, I'd go find Mort myself. But this time . . ." She let the words drift off.

"What's different about this time?"

"Mort's been scrimping and giving what little we had to Billy. Billy's in a bad way—or was. Now that he's in Albuquerque I'm sure he's found a source." Cara smiled weakly. "From the way he attacked you, I know it. The opium drives him bad crazy and he can't think straight. I reckon it's burned out his brain by now and turned him into more animal than man."

Slocum considered Billy Ferguson. While the attacks had seemed unprovoked, they were hardly those of a thoughtless animal. They had been carefully executed, even if Billy had missed both times.

The color in the man's cheeks, though, had returned to a normal hue. The pallor had gone and the burning intensity of the eyes told Slocum that Billy needed the drug just to maintain a semblance of a normal appearance.

That deathly white complexion marked Mort Thorogoode, too.

Slocum looked curiously at Cara. Her cheeks burned with rosiness, and she chewed at her lower lip in anguish over Thorogoode's fate.

"He's not had his opium for some time. How's that make it dangerous?" Slocum asked.

"Mort's likely to take too much to make up for the times he's missed. He doesn't like it when he gets the shakes and can't control himself. He flies off into wild rages, then becomes as docile as a lamb, then simply . . . fades away. He sits for hours staring at nothing. Then he's all right. For a while."

Cara started to cry. This time Slocum didn't try to comfort her.

"How can he afford it? Or Billy, for that matter," he added.

"It's not that expensive, John," she said in a tone that indicated she thought him a complete barbarian. "They can smoke a hundred pipes a day for only three or four dollars."

Slocum shook his head. For that kind of money he could live fairly well. Then he did the sums in his head.

"That could mean upwards of a thousand dollars a year," he said, startled at the huge amount. "Nobody spends that kind of money on smoking opium."

"Mort would, if the dope was always available," Cara answered.

He buckled on his gunbelt and checked the load in his Colt. For the next ten minutes, Slocum reloaded to make certain that the percussion caps and powder wouldn't fail him. All the time he tended his weapon, his mind raced. Seven different hop joints. Nosing around in any one of them would get him noticed. Within an hour every hophead in Albuquerque would be on the lookout for him.

Slocum decided against the straightforward approach of simply asking after Mort Thorogoode.

"Where's Billy likely to be?" he asked Cara. She sat quietly on one of the bunks watching him work. The question took her by surprise.

"I don't know. Down in the red light district, maybe. Near where you two fought."

"I'll start looking for him there. I doubt he got too far after I finished with him. He was going off like a whipped dog."

"Why do you want Billy?"

Slocum looked at her, trying to decide if he even ought to answer. "The pair of them probably found a place. If I find Billy, I'll probably find out where Mort is."

"Why not look for Mort and forget about Billy?"

Slocum wasn't finished with Billy Ferguson yet. Cara had interrupted them before he got full satisfaction. He rubbed his neck where the lynch mob had intended to drape their noose and remembered the feelings that had flooded his body when told to stand on the trapdoor high up on the gallows.

Billy had a lot more payment to give.

"I'll find Thorogoode. Don't you worry how."

Cara O'Connell looked uneasy at this. She motioned for him to stop, then dug around in a box and pulled out a wad of greenbacks. He silently took them and left the medicine-show wagon without a further word to the woman. He had a skunk to track down and the sooner he started, the sooner he'd be done.

Slocum walked back to the corner of Cooper and Third looking for Billy Ferguson. The area was similar to others he'd seen in his travelling through the West. This was the red light district, and anyone he met here would be suspicious of questions. The only people who ever asked more than simple directions carried the smell of the law to those gathered around.

"Welcome, stranger," called out a woman leaning in the doorway of an adobe building. "Is there anything I can do for you?" She lifted her skirt an indecent amount and gave Slocum a flash of bare thigh. The soiled dove moved her hips in a circular motion and licked her lips. Slocum went over to her.

"Might be something. I got a few dollars." He pulled out a couple of the bills Cara had given him and held them firmly. The way the whore's eyes lit up was almost pathetic.

"I got what you need, mister. I can give it all to you!"

She tried to pull him inside. He resisted, preferring to stay on the street. Twilight was beginning to settle, and the district had begun to churn with activity not present during the heat of the day.

"I'm looking for a friend," he said. Instant suspicion flared in the woman's dark eyes.

"Fuck off," she said, stepping back. Slocum added another bill to the two he held. She didn't want anything to do with him, but the lure of the money was more than she could bear.

Slocum described Billy Ferguson. "Where is he? One of the opium dens?"

"You want a flop and a *toy?*" she asked, her eyes blazing now with the same intense light Slocum had seen in both Thorogoode and Billy Ferguson. The whore must also be addicted to opium. Somehow, it didn't surprise him. "We got the best, right here in Hell's Half Acre."

Slocum had no idea what "a flop and a *toy*" were, but he nodded.

"I can show you. For a price." He handed over the bills, but the woman didn't stir. He added a final tattered bill from the wad Cara had given him for this rescue mission.

"I seen him. Not many passing through town this time of year. Not even a train for two days. He went over to Cuing's."

"Where's that?"

"I'll show you."

"You'll tell me." The coldness of his eyes caused the whore to step back half a pace and press herself into the dusty adobe wall.

"Between Copper and Railroad Avenue runs an alley. Just west of Fourth Street's where you'll find Cuing."

Slocum didn't say another word. She might have been lying to him, but he didn't think so. There had been fear in her voice, and just a hint of truth. Slocum found a one-story shanty made from rough-hewn planks. The slight wind caused the tent roof to flap and creak. Again came the odor of roasting peanuts—opium being smoked. Before he got around to the front, a movement out of the corner of his eye drew his attention. He saw Billy Ferguson hunched over and trying to sneak away. He stumbled and fell. By the time he'd gotten to his feet again, Slocum was there.

"Don't," whimpered Billy. "Don't hit me no more. I can't take it."

Slocum said nothing. The man looked a sight. Both eyes had blackened and the nose might have been broken. One cheek had swelled, and from the way he held his ribs, Slocum guessed he might have broken one or two.

"Tell me what I want to know and I'm done with you. Otherwise we'll have to have a long talk. A very long talk."

Billy's eyes darted left and right. There was no escape from Slocum.

"What do you want?" The words came out so low that Slocum almost missed them.

"Thorogoode. Where is he? With you, back in Cuing's?" That Slocum knew the name of the opium den's owner struck even more fear into Billy Ferguson.

THE JOURNEY OF DEATH 155

The man huddled on the ground, pulled his knees in to his chest, and shook his head. "Where is he, then?" demanded Slocum.

A heavy hand on Billy's collar pulled him erect. "We're going on a small tour of all the places where he might be," Slocum informed him. Billy struggled, but Slocum's grip on his collar was too strong. "We're going to have a good time together, unless you just happen to know which of these dens Thorogoode went to."

"Quong's," Billy choked out. "He said he was going to Quong's. B-but he might not have. I don't know!"

"Then we'll both find out for certain." Slocum remembered Cara had said Quong's was near Old Town. He oriented himself, decided that the central plaza was somewhere off to the northwest, and started walking, dragging Billy behind him like a reluctant mule.

"I don't want any part of this," Billy said. "I told you all I know. Let me go." The man's mental state had been affected by the opium he had smoked. Slocum saw the slow reflexes, the slurred speech, and the odd intensity to the eyes all marking him as being somehow different from most of the folks walking serenely along the plank sidewalks. While smoking, the hophead drifted off into a stupor. Afterward came heightened sensations and dulled physical reaction.

"What's a flop and a *toy?*"

"Fifty cents for a flop is about the usual. A dollar a *toy* around here." Slocum shook the man. Billy got the idea. "A flop's a bench to stretch out on when you're smoking. A *toy* is . . . a bone box with the opium in it. Maybe twenty pipes' worth of hop."

The adobe-walled church of San Felipe de Neri rose more than three stories on the north side of the plaza. Slocum circled the area, nose wrinkling for the slightest scent of opium. He found it on the southwest corner, about two blocks from the church. Slocum rapped smartly on the heavy wooden door.

"Who there?" came a muffled voice from inside.

"Friends," Slocum said. He pulled Billy up so that any unseen watchers could see that at least one of them was the right sort of client for an opium den.

The door opened on well-oiled hinges. Slocum ducked and went in, Billy trailing behind. The Celestial inside closed the door, bowed slightly, and silently gestured that they should proceed along the narrow corridor to the back of the building. The scent of burning opium made Slocum's head spin. He followed the Chinaman, who seemed to glide along like a ghost.

In the back room, Slocum stopped and peered into the smoky murk. Two dozen "flops" lined the walls and littered the floor space. Some had been curtained off for privacy, but most were exposed to the view of anyone entering. Slocum studied those reclining on the benches but failed to find Mort Thorogoode. Three of the curtained partitions were occupied; smoke rose from behind the dingy curtains and mingled with the smoke cloaking the rest of the room.

Slocum glanced around to determine what his chances were of opening the curtains and finding out who was behind those curtains. He decided his chances were poor. Men sat in tiny niches all around the perimeter of the room, shotguns across their laps. Two dozed off from the effect of the opium smoke, but two more looked alert for any trouble. Slocum wondered how often Quong allowed them to go out into the fresh air. Not often enough, from the looks of the first two—or maybe they were just getting ready to take a break.

Those other two guards looked mean enough to prevent any sort of trouble, especially among the physically debilitated hopheads.

"Three dollar," the Celestial said, pointing to a pair of vacant benches. Slocum silently paid. He had no intention of smoking, but any quibbling now would only cause further trouble. The guards eyed him and seemed to know he didn't belong.

"You first time?"

"For me. Not for him." Slocum saw how eagerly Billy flopped onto the bench and rolled onto his side, waiting.

"Easy. Velly, velly easy," the Chinaman assured Slocum. "You sit. I show."

The Celestial returned with a tray laden with a variety of arcane implements. He held up the pipe. Billy grabbed for it immediately.

"They call it a stem," Billy said. "You ought to try it, Slocum. Might do you some good. Relax you." The man awaited the next part of what amounted to a ritual.

The Celestial slowly unloaded the tray. An alcohol lamp and bowl cleaner were placed to one side. He held up a damp sponge. *"Souey pow,"* he said, "for creaning. And this is *yen hok.*"

"Use the needle to transfer the opium to the pipe," Billy said. His hands shook as he took the *yen hok* and rolled it around in the *toy* the Celestial opened. The bone box gleamed white and clean; inside rested the sticky black, tarry opium. A bead finally captured on the tip of the needle, Billy placed it into the bowl and waited.

The silent Oriental lit the alcohol lamp. Billy placed the pipe bowl over the flickering blue flame and nervously moved it to and fro, then inhaled deeply. Billows of smoke rose from both the bowl and out of Billy's nostrils. The man winced. Slocum had broken his nose, but the numbing effect of the opium did away with whatever pain he felt.

Slocum watched the stupefied expression cross Billy's face. Slackness caused the corner of his mouth to droop slightly and he drooled onto his chin. The Chinaman quickly wiped it away with the sponge.

"You tly now," he said, holding out the pipe for Slocum.

Slocum followed the ritual, knowing he dared not back out now. The guards watched him closely. He was the only one in the room not smoking heavily. He ran the needle through the molasses-like opium and held it in the pipe bowl. The Chinaman lit the lamp for him and waited. Slocum inhaled and held the smoke in his mouth, preventing it from getting into his lungs. The taste was fiercer than any quirly and burned tongue and nose. Slocum coughed and tears ran down his cheeks.

The Celestial's expression never changed, but Slocum sensed amusement. He took another draw on the pipe and controlled it better this time. A few more times and he lounged back, his head resting on the hard cushion, eyelids drooping. Even though he was keyed up, Slocum forced himself to go limp. He kept up a steady puffing, but he was nowhere near as incapacitated as Billy Ferguson.

Eyes half open, he watched all that went on in the room. The guards finally ignored him; he had become another hophead lost in opium stupor. Truth to tell, Slocum didn't feel any too alert. Even though he hadn't sucked the opium into his lungs, the air in the room was close and heavily laden with opium fumes. Simply being in the room gave more of the drug than he cared to take.

The two guards who'd been nodding off were awakened by the Celestial and chased from the room. Two more replaced them. Quong ran a tight opium den, with no trouble permitted.

Slocum tensed when one of the curtained partitions opened. The well-dressed man who rose from the fancier padded couch staggered slightly, then held out his hand. A woman who had been on a similar couch next to him stood. Hand in hand, they left the opium den. Eventually the other two partitioned-off couches disgorged their smokers. Neither was Mort Thorogoode.

Slocum considered the possibility that Billy had lied to him. The more likely answer was that Thorogoode moved around a good deal. Not one of the people other than Quong in this den of depravity was Chinese. Slocum figured that the Occidentals were the primary customers and that Thorogoode might drift from one to the other, either to feed his habit or to make contacts.

The people using the curtained couches were not guttersnipes or whores or petty thieves. They reeked of opium and money. Unless Slocum missed his guess, they were the ones who ran New Albuquerque.

Slocum sat up and shook Billy. Ferguson had smoked almost all of his *toy* of opium, while Slocum still had most of his left. "Come on, we're going. There are other places to try."

"Go 'way," Billy said in a slurred voice. The limpness of his body made Slocum think some master thief had robbed Billy of his skeleton and left only the skin. One bloodshot eye opened and peered up at Slocum. "Leave me 'lone."

"I have to find Thorogoode. You know where else he might be. Come on."

"No."

Slocum started to shake Billy when he saw the four guards sitting straighter and fingering the triggers of their shotguns. At first he thought he was the one responsible for this increased alertness, but it turned out that a newcomer had entered the den.

When Slocum saw who it was, he almost went for his gun. He mastered his first impulse and lay back down on the bench, pipe in his left hand, while his right rested near the butt of his pistol.

Henry Nathan strutted into the opium den.

"Damn, this is one fine place," Nathan proclaimed too loudly. One or two of the opium addicts stirred. Then they went back to their slow, deliberate puffing on their pipes. "I'm Henry Nathan and I rob banks. I want to spend some of the money I made here." He laughed as if he'd made the best joke in the world.

The muzziness Slocum had felt from the opium evaporated like mist in the hot morning sun. He concentrated on how much he wanted to get even with the backshooter who had left him for dead in the New Mexico desert. He had missed Nathan in Hot Springs and in Socorro, but he wouldn't miss him now.

Nathan dropped heavily to one of the couches on the far side of Billy Ferguson. Quong silently entered with the tray of implements and began laying them out. Nathan lay with his back to Slocum. From the way he handled the *yen hok*, Nathan was no stranger to the paraphernalia. He might not have used it many times before, but he knew what he was about.

Slocum waited until Quong had lit the small lamp and left Nathan happily puffing away at the opium before he made his move. He stood and stepped over Billy. Ferguson protested and this drew Nathan's attention.

Henry Nathan stared down the barrel of Slocum's Colt Navy. That .31 caliber turned into something bigger than the mouth of a cavern.

"Hello, Nathan," Slocum said quietly. He sat down, moving Billy away and keeping his eyes fixed on his quarry. "You got a lot to answer for."

"S-Slocum. But you got lynched for killing Nails!"

"I've been busy, too. But not as busy as you, from the looks of those duds." Nathan had outfitted himself in new clothes more fitting for the opera than for Albuquerque's streets. "Any of *my* money left?"

"I meant to cut you in, Slocum." Nathan's eyes darted from side to side, seeking a way out. Slocum's pistol never wavered from a spot just inches away from his heart. Nathan began to sweat.

"You meant to shotgun me and leave me in the desert to die. But I didn't. Larouche couldn't kill me. Rawlinson couldn't. You can't. And now you got all the money from the bank."

"Don't shoot me."

"Persuade me. The money is a good start."

Nathan licked his dried lips. "If I give you the money, you'll gun me down."

"Most likely," Slocum said. "The money doesn't mean warm spit to me compared with seeing you dead. But it might buy me off. Might not, but it just may be the only way you'll ever live to double-cross anyone again."

Nathan started to shout to the guards, but stopped when Slocum cocked the Colt. Even if Slocum had been in the opium den all day long, there was no way he could miss at such close range. Nathan quieted down.

"What'samatter, Slocum?" demanded Billy. "What you sittin' on me for like that?"

The man turned and jostled Slocum's gun arm. Nathan moved like lightning, the needle holding a tiny bead of opium lancing straight for Slocum's face. Slocum ducked and felt the sharp tip sear his skin. He fired and knew he missed even as he did so. Nathan had twisted and dropped to the opium den's dirty floor.

The gunshot drew the four guards like shit draws flies. Their shotguns came up and the hammers pulled back. By this time Nathan had his gun out and was firing wildly.

Slocum winced as two of the shotguns erupted with leaden death. Henry Nathan's body exploded into a red mist before his eyes. A third shotgun's barrel ruptured under its load. The guard who was holding it started cursing volubly.

Billy Ferguson jerked upright, not sure of what was happening. Slocum saw the fourth guard begin to turn. He made a grab for Billy and missed by scant inches. The first load caught Ferguson squarely in the chest. The man tumbled back over a low couch and lay spread-eagled on the floor, his chest turned to sausage.

The smoke from the gunpowder and the opium turned the the room into a murky swamp of shifting clouds. Slocum fired once and heard the guard grunt. Metallic clicks and snaps told of the others reloading. Slocum wiggled on his belly to the door and kicked through as another hail of pellets sought him out. The wooden door to the room exploded into toothpicks.

"Don't," Slocum said, his pistol pointing directly at Quong. The Celestial stood by the main door to the opium den, hands hidden inside the voluminous sleeves of his robe. "Pull those hands out slow so I can see them."

A wicked knife with a gleaming foot-long blade slowly appeared. Slocum motioned for the Chinaman to toss it into a side room. Only when it clanked on the brick floor did Slocum approach Quong.

"Let me out of here. Now!"

The thudding of heavy boots against the floor in the opium-smoking room told Slocum he had only seconds to get away before all hell broke loose. He couldn't survive a prolonged fight against two, maybe three men armed with shotguns—not in these cramped quarters, not with so many drugged bystanders to hinder him. The guards had no compunction against gunning down anybody in their way.

Quong bowed slightly and pulled back the wooden bar across the heavy outer door. Slocum slipped into the cool, clean air of the desert night, his lungs heaving. Sweat evaporated quickly from his body, but he quickly worked up a new sweat—this time from exertion.

Quong's singsongy instructions from inside the opium den to the guards had been to kill him. Slocum wanted to put as much distance between them and him as he could.

When he reached Railroad Avenue, he slowed to a brisk walk and reholstered his gun. He heaved a sigh when he saw no sign of pursuit.

But Billy Ferguson had died a messy death in the opium parlor. And so had Henry Nathan, taking with him the secret of where he'd hidden the money from the bank robbery. Slocum closed his eyes for a moment, reflected on what a bitch it had been over the past few weeks, then shook himself and began walking for the east side of town. Not much had gone right this evening, and telling Frieda that her husband was dead only added to the things that rankled.

13

Slocum stood at the corner of Railroad Avenue and First and let the wind whip away the sweat that had been beading his forehead. He tried not to be too obvious as he looked around, sure that everyone passing him in the street knew where he had been and what he'd just gone through. No one took the slightest notice, but Slocum's nerves approached the breaking point.

Someone stalked him. He had left the opium den at a dead run, pulling up to a brisk walk when it had seemed that Quong had not ordered any of the guards after him. Now Slocum wasn't so sure. The "itch" he felt when tracking told him he was someone's prey.

He turned off Railroad Avenue and momentarily abandoned the idea of returning to Doctor Denton's Marvelous Travelling Medicine Show, at least until he made sure he wasn't being tracked down like a wounded buck.

The meat clever crashed into the post beside his head, sending splinters flying into the darkness. Slocum ducked instinctively and swung about, gun in hand. He faced a sallow Chinaman who struggled to pull his weapon out of the wood where he had half buried the wicked blade.

"Don't," Slocum said. His fingers tightened on the Colt's trigger when it became apparent the Celestial wasn't going to obey. Slocum hesitated. The man might not understand English. Slocum decided it didn't matter; the Chinaman had to be stopped or he would eventually succeed in burying that cleaver in his head.

The Celestial jerked the cleaver free just as Slocum fired. The gunshot echoed along the street, causing people to stop and look around. In the distance came the clatter of a horse-drawn trolley which drowned out the Celestial's death moan. Slocum stood over the robed Chinaman and stared at the slack face.

"Who the hell are you?" he wondered aloud. It wasn't Quong, so it had to be one of Quong's men. Slocum quickly decided that if Quong had sent one, there'd be another—and another, and maybe even more than this. Leaving New Albuquerque as quick as he could seemed the only safe course to follow.

It still rankled that Henry Nathan had died without revealing where the bank money had been hidden. It bothered Slocum even more than some nameless, faceless guard in an opium den had been the one to kill Nathan. For all the man had done, Slocum had wanted that pleasure for himself.

"Dead's dead," he muttered to himself, casting one last look down at the Chinaman. "Still wish Nathan had come into my gunsights, though." Slocum slipped back into the street and got an even stronger feeling of eyes watching now—unfriendly eyes. He turned and retreated into the cloaking darkness of the alley connecting Railroad Avenue with Mountain Road.

He hurried north, skirting the Old Town plaza. The crunch of gravel and occasional rustling of leather against hips told him at least four men were closing in on him. Slocum dodged and ducked, moved and tried to lay a false trail. In the mountains he would have circled on them with no problem. A forest would have given him ample opportunity to lay a trap. But he was out of his element. Albuquerque didn't provide the kinds of diversions Slocum was used to.

He cursed all cities and vowed to get out of this and hightail it for the mountains. The Rockies to the west of Denver became more and more attractive by the moment.

"There he is," came a voice barely audible over the hundred yards separating Slocum and his trackers. He watched as four distinct shadows moved closer. They had spotted him. He would either have to make a stand and fight or try to outrun them. Slocum had never believed in needlessly dying, but turning tail and running was the coward's way out.

He leveled his pistol, sighted carefully, and fired. The tongue of flame from the muzzle leaped out more than three feet. The lead slug crashed into one of the men. He let out a tiny sound somewhere between a curse and a whimper before sagging motionless to the ground. The other three dived for cover.

Then all hell broke loose.

Two carried shotguns. The third had a rifle. Slocum found himself pinned down behind a stack of crates piled near a millinery store's rear door. He tried to work to the door and break it down to escape through the hat store, but accurate fire from the man with the rifle prevented it. Slocum had to duck for cover repeatedly.

He peered out to see one of the men with a shotgun bobbing and twisting as he moved to a new position. They intended putting him into a crossfire. If that happened, Slocum knew he was a goner. He craned his head around and peered up. If he couldn't move along the alley or get through the door, that was the only way left for him.

It didn't look promising. The brick building left scant footing for him to get to the roof. At the corner he saw a drainpipe, but it was too far away to do him any good. A blast from one shotgun ripped apart the front of the crate he used for protection. Slocum had to fall belly-down and wiggle to another. Another blast filled the night's silence and a hot lead pellet creased his upper arm.

Slocum didn't have to peek out to know what he next sound he heard was: the other man with the shotgun shifted position. They were in as good a position now as they would ever be. With the shotguns on either side of the alley and the rifleman in the middle, they commanded his every escape. Sooner or later, one would get a good shot at him.

Slocum cursed Mort Thorogoode, then cursed Billy Ferguson, and finally started in on Cara O'Connell. Without her gentle persuasions he might not have found himself in this alley. Riding north to the salvation offered by wide-open spaces took on more importance by the instant, but it was still a distant second to simply staying alive.

Slocum shifted position again when another pair of shotgun blasts ripped apart a crate to his left. He pressed his back against the cool brick wall and held his Colt ready in case the men out there got itchy and rushed him. It would be stupid for them to do that when all they had to do was wait him out, but he had to be prepared. His training in the War had taught him never to take anything for granted.

He pressed back against the wall even more when a rifle bullet sang its song of death just inches from his head. The sharpshooter had no clear target; he had only guessed where Slocum might be. That didn't make Slocum feel any better.

But what his fingers found behind him did. He dropped back to his belly and shoved the crate forward. Revealed was a small window leading to a cellar. Whoever had built this brick store must have come from back East.

The only reason for cellars was protection from tornadoes and for storage. Why it had been built didn't matter to Slocum. That it was here might save him. He fumbled and cursed and fought and finally levered the balky window open far enough to crawl through. Before he dropped into the cellar, he carefully fired three shots in the direction of the man with the rifle.

"Ought to keep him honest, for a while, at least," Slocum muttered. He dropped into the shallow cellar and found he couldn't even straighten up. His head brushed the floor of the shop. Slocum stumbled and blundered through the box-laden cellar the best he could. A small trap door opened into the milliner's shop. Slocum squirmed from the basement and got behind a counter. He took the time to reload—and waited.

He hadn't misjudged the men after him. They were no fools. They had figured out not only that he had vanished but where he'd gone. Slocum walked on silent feet to the door and forced it open. He left it standing slightly ajar, then went back behind the counter, crouched down and alert. The first head through the trap in the floor slowly swiveled, taking in everything. When the man spotted the opened front door, he hoisted himself up and called out, "He left by the front way. Get around. One of you go to the north end of the block, the other south. Hurry up, damn it!"

Slocum saw that this man carried a rifle—the man he had pegged as being the leader. Shooting him down would be easy. Slocum had no compunction about doing it, but he needed to know who was after him and what it would take to call off the hounds.

Just as the man got to the front door, Slocum propped his Colt on the counter and said, "Drop the rifle. Make one move I don't like, and you end up sucking wind through a new hole in your head."

The rifleman obeyed. The Winchester clattered as it hit the floor.

"Is it Quong?" Slocum asked. "He the one who sent you?"

"Quong," the rifleman confirmed. "He don't like it when his guards get shot up. Can't say I do, either." The man stiffened, waiting for the slug to rip apart his spine. The bullet never came. "You gonna wait me to death?"

"I got no quarrel with Quong," said Slocum. "What would it take to settle accounts with him?"

The man turned and stared open-mouthed at Slocum. "Be damned," he said. "Never heard of anyone wanting to dicker, especially when they had the drop on me. What's your game, mister?"

"Don't like killing for no reason."

"Charlie's deader'n shit. That's more than no reason."

Outside Slocum heard the soft movement of the two men with the shotguns closing in from either end of the block. His mind raced and he saw no easy way out of his dilemma. He couldn't let them kill him, but he didn't cotton to the idea of killing them, either. He'd seen too much wanton murder in his day. Hell, Nathan's shooting up the bank in El Paso del Norte had started this.

"Out. Into the street. Now!"

The man turned and bolted. He ran out, shouting, but the words vanished in the double roar of shotguns. Both men gunned down their boss. Slocum scooped up the fallen Winchester and waited. The two ran up, triumphant. The one to the north figured out first what they'd done.

"Jesus," he muttered. "That's not the one we wanted. It's Watters. We killed Watters!"

The idea hit both men at the same time that Slocum still had to be in the shop. They swung their shotguns around, barrels coming up. Slocum picked off the one on the left with the Winchester, dropped the rifle, and finished the job with his Colt. It took three shots before the gunman on the right lay in the street, unmoving.

Slocum's gut churned. It had been too long since he'd

been caught up in killing like this. He'd forgotten how much it sickened him. He took a deep breath, closed his eyes, and waited for another sensation to work its way through to his brain.

Alone. He was alone in the street. No more of Quong's men on his trail. Slocum turned back east toward the nightshrouded Sandia Mountains and the place where the medicine show had camped.

Slocum stopped when he caught sight of the gaudy wagon. Something wasn't quite right, and he didn't immediately know what it was. It finally came to him that there was a deserted feel to the wagon. Billy Ferguson would never be returning here, and he doubted Thorogoode had blundered back. But Cara ought to be here.

He approached and peered into the wagon. A small lantern cast its pale yellow light onto the walls. No one was inside. Slocum's quick eyes sought out some sign of struggle, an indication Cara had been dragged away unwillingly. He saw nothing to indicate she hadn't just wandered off.

Slocum spun, gun in hand, when he heard movement behind. He checked himself when he recognized Frieda Ferguson.

"No need for that, John," the woman said in a tired voice. "Or maybe it'd just put me out of my misery."

"Where's Cara?"

Frieda shrugged. "She just went off. Like Billy, like Mort. Just went . . . off."

Slocum started to tell the woman that her husband lay dead on the floor of an opium den, then stopped. She hadn't been far wrong when she had mentioned her misery. The haunted look turned her face gaunt and added a dozen years to her age. While her eyes appeared dry, tiny tracks in the dust on her cheeks showed where she'd been crying. For Billy? For herself?

Slocum couldn't bring himself to tell her about Billy Ferguson.

"When did Cara leave?" he asked.

"You find Mort?"

"Did Cara go looking for him on her own?" Slocum asked. "I've been looking but I haven't found him. I don't think she'd have much luck on her own."

The woman's harsh laughter startled him.

"What do you know about her that I don't?" he demanded.

"Cara's a hophead, too. Just like Mort. Just like my Billy. Not as bad, maybe, but she takes her share of opium."

Slocum said nothing. He just stared at Frieda. She moved listlessly and perched on the bare stage, staring up into the sky. The stars winked back at her, their coldness rivalling what Slocum felt in his guts.

"Cara's been trying to stop Mort from using so much opium, but he won out, the son of a bitch. He won out. He got her to try it. There was no looking back for her then. She had to have more. Don't know what that evil black filth does to a person, but it makes them over. Turns them into its slave."

Frieda turned and looked at Slocum. "The War was supposed to free the slaves. It might have freed some. But not the likes of Mort or Cara. Or Billy Ferguson."

"Did she know where Thorogoode was?" Slocum asked. He didn't like the idea of being sent on a wild goose chase. Or even worse, sent to track down a likely opium parlor for a female hophead.

Frieda shook her head. "She's worried about Mort. I heard what she told you. All true. I think if Mort gets enough this time it might just do him in. He's been taking too much of his own medicines over the years. He has spells where he can't control himself. Breathing gets labored and he falls down. Claims the opium helps it, but it doesn't. Makes it even worse."

"When did Cara leave?"

"Maybe an hour ago. Not more'n two. I ain't got any

idea where she is, and you know something, John? I don't rightly care. I got worries of my own. It's bad waitin' for Billy to get back. Drunk or crazy out of his head from the opium, it doesn't matter to me. I just want him back."

"What if he never came back?" The coldness inside turned arctic in its intensity. Slocum had now and again been the one to tell brothers and cousins and uncles and nephews of a relative's death during the War. He'd never had to tell a wife or mother or sister. It was even harder, he discovered.

Frieda stared at him. Tears welled up. She brushed them away almost guiltily. "Then I won't have to wait up for him. Is he dead, John? Is that what you're telling me?"

"He died in an opium den. One of the guards—"

Frieda held up a hand to silence him. "I don't care for the details. He won't be coming back. That's the important part. That's the only part that matters." She swung her stocky legs up to the stage, stood, and went into the wagon. The door closed quietly behind her. Only then did Slocum hear the wracking sobs.

He sat down, feeling awful.

His horse whinnied and tugged at its tether. Slocum went over and soothed the animal, stroking over its long head and patting it on the neck. "Old fella, if I had a lick of sense I'd saddle you up and we'd ride to Santa Fe without stopping. But that's supposing I had a lick of sense."

Slocum felt no sense of duty to Mort Thorogoode or even Cara O'Connell now, but in an odd way he owed Frieda Ferguson something. He hadn't been the one who had killed Billy—but he would have, given the chance. Billy Ferguson was a backshooting, conniving son of a bitch who didn't deserve a wife like Frieda. No, he hadn't killed Billy, nor had he been directly responsible for it.

But he owed Frieda. He'd find Thorogoode and Cara

and get them back to the medicine show. It was all any of them truly had in the world. He'd bring them back and that would end it for him. Any obligation he had would be fully discharged.

He settled his gunbelt around his hips, made sure the Colt rode easy in the cross-draw holster, and went looking for Cara O'Connell.

14

Slocum had no desire to go hunting through the opium dens now that Quong had decided to remove future problems. The thought of the men who'd died already chilled Slocum. Why had they died? There seemed no good reason other than that Quong wanted him dead and had misjudged how much trouble that might be.

The den closest to where the medicine wagon had stopped was down near the Alvarado Hotel, just a few blocks from the railyards. In the distance Slocum heard a mournful train whistle. Even on a spur from Lamy, not many trains came this way. There wasn't anything but desert to the south, and if anyone wanted to go to San Francisco they would have to go north through Salt Lake City.

Slocum made his way along the wide streets and sniffed out the opium den. His inclination was to forget the whole sordid mess and leave. What could he really accomplish now? The answer to that was vague as Slocum slipped past the hanging canvas curtain that served as a door and

173

into the dimly lit interior. The now familiar fragrance of opium being smoked rose to his nostrils. He wanted to gag.

The room was almost identical to that in Quong's smoking room. What struck Slocum even more was the clientele. All white, all fairly rich-looking, not an Oriental to be seen. The Chinamen seemed to export their vices well. The man running the den came over to Slocum and slapped him on the shoulder.

"Welcome, mister. You interested in a little happy smoke?"

Slocum indicated one of the partitioned-off couches. If Cara O'Connell was anywhere, this was the place. No woman was in sight in the more public areas.

"Don't want to look at all the down-and-outs, eh?" the man said, mistaking Slocum's intent. "Come right this way. We'll have you fixed up with a *toy* in just a minute."

Slocum ripped back the cloth curtain hiding the occupant of the hidden couch. The man running the opium den spun, dark anger rising on his face.

"It's all right," came the slow, drugged words. "He's with me." Cara O'Connell sprawled on a cushioned couch, her eyes half closed and the smoker's characteristic slackness in her face turning her beauty into something hideous.

"Whatever you say," the man said, but he didn't leave. Slocum handed him a couple of the bills Cara had given him earlier to use in finding Thorogoode. This produced the desired result; the man drifted off to tend to his other patrons.

Slocum pulled the curtain back around and sat on the edge of the couch.

"You're wondering why," Cara said slowly.

"Thorogoode got you started."

"Mort did," she said, "but I wanted to keep doing it. The smoke makes me forget everything. Makes me feel good. Makes me feel like a queen!"

"How bad is it?"

"It's not bad, John darling. It's wonderful! When I don't have it isn't good, but I don't need it like Mort and Billy. They have a real yen that even smoking all day can hardly cure."

"Billy's dead." He said it harshly, to shock her. The blonde barely stirred on the couch.

"Had to happen sooner or later. Billy was a loser. Does Frieda know?"

"I told her."

"Poor Frieda." Slocum thought Cara meant Frieda losing her husband. Then Cara said, "She'll never know how good it is smoking opium. She doesn't even take laudanum."

Slocum started to slap Cara, then stopped. As drugged as she was, even the sharp sting of pain wouldn't bring her around to a more coherent condition. He knocked the pipe from her lax fingers when she started to inhale again. Before Cara could protest, he jerked her upright and got an arm around her for support. She protested feebly, not wanting to leave. Slocum drew back the dirty curtain and found the owner of the opium den standing there. For a split second, Slocum thought the man was going to protest. He read the fury in Slocum's green eyes and backed off.

Outside, the cool night breezes did little to arouse Cara. She stumbled and staggered under the opium's powerful influence. Slocum saw a watering trough and threw the woman in it. His heart almost stopped when she stayed face down under the water. He thought she'd passed out and was getting ready to drown. Just before he would have pulled her out, Cara struggled free on her own.

"What'd you do that for?" she asked with a bit more animation in her voice.

He shoved her back into the trough.

This time, she came out wet and angry. "Stop that! You're ruining my gown. This cost three hundred dollars in San Francisco!"

Slocum could believe it. The expensive dress had been ruined by the water, but he counted it as a small loss getting Cara into a condition where he could talk to her.

"Billy's dead, I can't find Thorogoode, and Frieda's back in the wagon. Seven or eight men have been killed because I went looking for Thorogoode, and I'm not about to keep up the hunt. You find him or not. I don't care."

Cara O'Connell began to cry. The tears leaked soundlessly from her eyes and ran down her cheeks. No sobs, no moans, just tears.

"John, I can't help myself. I'm so weak. I knew I could never get Mort out of an opium den by myself. I'd join him and we'd spend the rest of the night together smoking. That's the real reason I asked you to get him."

"But you couldn't stay away."

"No. I'm so ashamed of my weakness, but I can't help it. It chews away inside me. I *need* it. I get awful hot flashes and tremble and then fall asleep."

"I saw what happened to Thorogoode and Billy." Cara's addiction explained her paleness, too. She covered it well with rouge on the cheeks and the other makeup used for the medicine-show act, but it wouldn't be much longer before her beauty vanished altogether because of the insidious effects of the drug.

"Find Mort. Please, John. I don't want him out there. I don't want to be out there." The tears continued to flow.

"Come on." He helped her up and and they went back to the wagon. He helped her sit on the stage and stared straight into her slightly glazed eyes. "Are you going to give up the opium smoking?" he flat-out asked.

Cara shook her head. "I don't think I can." She hung her head and for the first time really began to sob and cry.

Slocum pushed her away. "I'll find Thorogoode for you. But that's all."

"John, I love you!"

Slocum spun and started off down Railroad Avenue. The entire street was abuzz with activity, people huddled in small clusters eagerly exchanging gossip. A small boy had a stack of single-sheet newspapers and called out, "Git yer extra. Git yer *Morning Journal* and find out about the opium murders. Hurry, they're goin' fast!"

Slocum slipped the boy two pennies and quickly scanned the extra. It was pretty much as he'd guessed. The marshal had gotten riled over so many murders in the opium dens. The city fathers had protested the violence and demanded—again—the closing of the parlors. A ripple of concern ran through Hell's Half Acre, as the prostitutes and gamblers and madams were sure they would be the next ones slaughtered.

Nowhere did the article mention Quong or Billy Ferguson.

Slocum crumpled the paper and tossed it away. Where was he going to find Mort Thorogoode, especially now that the law patrolled the opium dens? Almost as if his wish had been granted, Slocum heard loud arguing down the street. He peered out and saw Thorogoode struggling with the marshal.

Boldness counted for more than anything else now. Slocum hopped off the sidewalk and into the street and quickly strode to where Thorogoode was complaining about his treatment at the hands of New Albuquerque's lawman.

"... no way to treat Doctor Denton!"

"I'll Doctor Denton you, you hophead," the marshal said. He shook Thorogoode so hard the man's teeth audibly rattled. "You hit one of my deputies."

"Marshal, pardon me," cut in Slocum. "What seems to be the problem?"

"No problem. Unless you want to make one. Butt out."

Before the marshal could swing Thorogoode around and hustle him off to jail, Slocum said, "This man is my employer. I'm a handyman for the travelling medicine show. I wouldn't want him to spend the night in jail. Can we come to some sort of an agreement so's Doctor Denton can sleep in his own bed this night?"

The marshal gave Slocum a once-over, but no flicker of recognition lit his eyes. "That true?" the marshal demanded of Thorogoode. "This man work for you?"

"Indeed, he does. I have performed many feats of . . ."

"Shut up," the marshal said dispassionately. To Slocum, he said, "All right. I don't want to lock him up. Got too damn many in the cells now. But I don't want him runnin' loose and gettin' into any more trouble."

"I know of his affliction," said Slocum. "He won't trouble you again."

"Affliction, hell. The son of a bitch is an opium smoker. Sweat that out of him after three months in jail."

"What did he do?"

"Got smoked up and tore apart Clyde's grain store. Spilled oats and barley and what-all onto the floor and stomped on it. Seemed to think it was bugs or something." The marshal spat and accurately hit a post with his tobacco gob. "Done close to fifty dollars' damage. Got to have that paid off before I can let him go."

Slocum pried the bills from his pocket. He hadn't bothered counting them when Cara had given them to him earlier. Sixty was all that was left. He kept thinking how much he longed for this money. This was more scrip than he'd seen in well nigh four months. It might be more than his share of the El Paso del Norte bank robbery. He should have forgotten about Thorogoode and ridden north. But he hadn't.

The marshal's quick appraisal took in every penny of the wad. "Then there's a ten-dollar fine for disturbing the peace." Slocum silently handed over the crumpled greenbacks. The marshal tucked them into his shirt pocket and shoved Thorogoode into Slocum's arms.

"He's all yours."

"This . . . this beast robbed me!" declared Thorogoode.

Slocum spun him around, not bothering to be gentle. He wanted to be away from the marshal before the man decided Slocum had something to do with all the furor in the opium dens. There had to be a description circulating.

"He took all my money," said Thorogoode. "You can't let him do that!"

"It's for the best, Thorogoode. You can't spend any more on opium. I'm taking you back to the wagon where you can sleep this off." Slocum felt as if every eye in Albuquerque followed them as they slowly returned to the medicine wagon. The marshal would be pressured into closing down the opium dens for a while, and this would only make the owners even angrier. If Quong was willing to send out men to gun him down over a couple of deaths inside the opium den, losing the revenue for even a day would make the Chinaman even madder. He'd have the entire populace of Hell's Half Acre out looking for Slocum, all ready to shoot him where he stood.

"Billy's dead," Slocum said harshly. "I suppose you knew that."

"I heard," said Thorogoode. "We smoked earlier at Quong's."

Slocum hesitated then. Billy hadn't been lying when he had said Thorogoode was likely to be in the opium den. He and Thorogoode had been there together before Slocum found Billy.

"Strange," muttered Thorogoode. "Seldom seen such a sight."

"What are you talking about? I figure you and Ferguson went out a lot."

"In the opium den. We had just finished our first pipe when a bank robber came in."

Slocum swung Thorogoode around and pinned him against the side of the wagon. "What did he look like? Scarred face, dark eyes?"

"Henry Nathan, yes, that's the name. He bragged on and on about how dangerous a man he was. He began smoking on the couch next to ours." Thorogoode began giggling like a schoolgirl. "Funny. It struck me as funny. A bank robber smoking opium."

"What's so funny about that?"

"He brought his own with him. Thought he did. About the right size."

"What was the right size?" Slocum began to lose his temper.

"The package. What else do you bring to an opium den besides money? But he left it when he went. Too much opium to remember, I reckon."

Slocum asked, "This was at Quong's? Which couch did Nathan use?"

Thorogoode's mind had found another trail and followed it. He went on and on about how the moon looked like a tarnished dime in the sky and how the U. S. Mint should do something about it. Slocum pulled him onto the stage at the rear of the wagon and rapped sharply on the door. After almost a minute Cara O'Connell opened the door. She didn't seem to understand why Slocum had returned; Slocum figured this was the effect of the opium still holding her senses captive. Then she saw Thorogoode.

"Mort! Oh, John, thank you. You found him."

"Cost me the rest of the money you gave me."

"You found him." Cara cradled Thorogoode's head in her lap and rocked him as if he were a babe in arms. He stared down and made his decision. Without a word to Cara, he dropped off the stage and headed back into town again. Slocum snorted in disgust. He was going to be making this trip so many times he'd need a new pair of boots.

Slocum skirted Railroad Avenue and the uneasiness there and kept to the quieter back streets. He found his way to Old Town and immediately spotted deputy marshals walking a slow patrol, rifles carried in the crooks of their arms. The marshal had shut down the entire area, and probably had confiscated everything in Quong's opium den.

Slocum drifted like a ghost through the plaza and came out behind Quong's. He heard faint voices at the front. He moved around on silent feet and found a spot where he could eavesdrop.

"Not enough, Quong. They want your stinking yellow hide," the marshal said. "Can't say's I blame them, either. Christ, how'd you let it get out of hand like this? Eight men dead, six of them yours."

"Outraw. The one was Nathan the bank lobber."

"That ought to quiet some of the citizens," the marshal said. "Look. I'll close you down for another week. By then everyone'll have forgot about this. That's the best I can do."

"No pay blibe."

"You damn well will!" raged the marshal. "You'll pay me or you'll never open up again."

The wrangling went on, but Slocum paid scant attention. The bribes paid to the marshal by Quong and the other owners of the opium dens were of little interest— or not as much interest as the idea that everything inside the opium parlor went untouched. All the marshal had said was that he had shut it down, not confiscated the contents.

Slocum found a window ledge and climbed up onto it. Spanish architecture didn't allow for a window large enough to crawl through, but it gave him a foot up to where he caught a projecting end of a *viga*. He grabbed the thick wooden support and pulled himself onto the flat roof. Slocum kept low and tried not to make too much noise as he searched the roof for a spot directly over the opium-smoking room below. The constant higher heat in the room came to his aid. As if someone had burned an outline on the roof, he knew where his goal was.

A weak spot in the roof, a small vent hole, and fifteen minutes of silent, frantic work, and Slocum dropped into the opium den. He felt as if he had fallen into the Black Hole of Calcutta. The darkness was absolute and the stench overwhelmed Slocum. He staggerred slightly, fighting for breath. He was forced to sit on one of the couches until the dizziness passed. The air in the closed room had taken on a potent touch from so much opium being smoked.

Slocum listened for any indication that he'd been heard. Nothing. Fumbling about blindly, he kicked over an alcohol lamp. He made a grab for it and got it before it rolled away. With great deliberation, he found a lucifer in his pocket, struck it, and in the brilliant flare found the wick of the lamp.

The dancing blue flame was almost painful to his eyes but it gave the light Slocum needed to poke around in the room. The first thing he did was check the door leading to the hallway and the rest of the building. It had been repaired and securely barred on the outside. Anyone trying to get in would have to make a racket loud enough to awaken the dead. Slocum relaxed a bit more. He had a free hand in searching the room.

While it might have been Thorogoode's opium-demented mind that conjured up Henry Nathan's presence here, Slocum didn't think so. Nathan hadn't been *coming* to Quong's, he had been *returning*. And Thorogoode mentioned seeing a small package. There was only one item Slocum could think of that Nathan wouldn't let out of his sight: the money from the bank robbery.

He started searching the couches in a random fashion, going from one to the other. Mostly he found nothing but dirt and rat droppings under the couches. Slocum heaved a deep breath, regretted it as the lingering opium

worked on his brain and body, then started a more me-
thodical search. After nine of the wooden flops he found
a small parcel wrapped in oilskin.

Fingers trembling with excitement, he peeled away
the cloth. In the blue flame of the lamp he saw a small
stack of greenbacks. Slocum knew better than to sit and
count the money, but he did anyway.

Four hundred dollars. It hardly seemed enough for
surviving the El Paso del Norte bank robbery, surviving
Nathan's shotgun blast, surviving all that had happened
as a result. But if it had been four thousand dollars Slocum wasn't sure it would have paid him back. He belonged out in the mountains, where he could feel free.
What price could he ever hope to pay for that feeling?
For him, the open sky and endless range and towering,
purple-hazed mountains were like Cara's opium was to
her. This money was only a way of getting there.

He tucked the greenbacks into the front of his shirt,
then moved two of the couches together so that he could
climb back through the hole in the roof. He pulled himself
out into the crisp desert night and let the untainted air
sink to the bottom of his lungs and flush out all the opium
he had inhaled unwittingly.

Only then did Slocum make a slow circuit of the roof
to check for guards. One of the deputies stood out front.
Other than this solitary sentry, the way was clear. He
dropped off the building in the back and almost ran to
the medicine show.

The lamps were lit inside and the back door was open.
Slocum stared at the warm yellow light spilling out and
thought of Cara. Then he went to where his horse stood
patiently. He got his tack, saddled, and climbed up. As
he did so he heard the wooden stage at the back of the
wagon creak with someone's weight.

"John? Is that you?"

Slocum felt a pang of sorrow for Cara O'Connell. She
wanted away from the life of the travelling medicine

show, yet she needed it more than life itself. Without the opium she would wither and turn into a husk of her lovely self.

With it, she'd simply die.

"You're not leaving, John. You can't. Wait!"

Against his better judgment, Slocum found himself riding slowly over to look Cara in the eye. The obvious effects of the opium had passed now. A lovely, desirable woman held her hand out to him, touched his cheek. The horse shied away enough to take him beyond her reach.

"You got Thorogoode back," he said in a flat voice.

"John, take me with you. Let me..." Cara's voice trailed off. She smiled ruefully and shook her head. "No, that would never work out for either of us, would it?"

"No, it wouldn't."

She held out her hand again. Slocum leaned over. Their lips lightly brushed and then Cara stepped back.

"Goodbye, John." A tear sparkled in the corner of her eye.

Slocum put his heels into the horse's flanks and trotted off. He sighted the Big Dipper and found the Pole Star. Getting to Santa Fe would be easy enough now that he knew where he was heading.

Doctor Wong's—or Doctor Denton's, or whatever it would be called next—Travelling Medicine Show vanished into the night behind him without a trace, without a regret.

GREAT WESTERN YARNS FROM ONE OF THE BEST-SELLING WRITERS IN THE FIELD TODAY

JAKE
LOGAN

JAKE LOGAN

___ 0-867-21087	**SLOCUM'S REVENGE**	$1.95
___ 07296-3	**THE JACKSON HOLE TROUBLE**	$2.50
___ 07182-0	**SLOCUM AND THE CATTLE QUEEN**	$2.75
___ 06413-1	**SLOCUM GETS EVEN**	$2.50
___ 06744-0	**SLOCUM AND THE LOST DUTCHMAN MINE**	$2.50
___ 07018-2	**BANDIT GOLD**	$2.50
___ 06846-3	**GUNS OF THE SOUTH PASS**	$2.50
___ 07046-8	**SLOCUM AND THE HATCHET MEN**	$2.50
___ 07258-4	**DALLAS MADAM**	$2.50
___ 07139-1	**SOUTH OF THE BORDER**	$2.50
___ 07460-9	**SLOCUM'S CRIME**	$2.50
___ 07567-2	**SLOCUM'S PRIDE**	$2.50
___ 07382-3	**SLOCUM AND THE GUN-RUNNERS**	$2.50
___ 07494-3	**SLOCUM'S WINNING HAND**	$2.50
___ 08382-9	**SLOCUM IN DEADWOOD**	$2.50

Prices may be slightly higher in Canada.

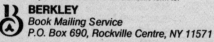